The Best
That You
Can Do

ALSO BY AMINA GAUTIER

The Loss of All Lost Things

Now We Will Be Happy

At-Risk

The Best That You Can Do

◇ Stories ◇

AMINA GAUTIER

Soft Skull
New York

The Best That You Can Do

Library of Congress Cataloging-in-Publication Data
Names: Gautier, Amina, 1977– author.
Title: The best that you can do : stories / Amina Gautier.
Other titles: Best that you can do (Compilation)
Description: First Soft Skull edition. | New York : Soft Skull, 2024.
Identifiers: LCCN 2023035035 | ISBN 9781593767587 (trade paperback) | ISBN 9781593767655 (ebook)
Subjects: LCSH: Puerto Rican families—Fiction. | Puerto Ricans—Fiction. | LCGFT: Short stories.
Classification: LCC PS3607.A976 B47 2024 | DDC 813/.6—dc23/eng/20230804
LC record available at https://lccn.loc.gov/2023035035

Cover design by Farjana Yasmin
Cover photo © iStock / kkong5
Book design by Laura Berry

Published by Soft Skull Press
New York, NY
www.softskull.com

Printed in the United States of America

1 3 5 7 9 10 8 6 4 2

Contents

◊

Breathe

Quarter Rican

What She Finds

What she finds on the rooftop is her friend Inez's brother, sitting quietly on an upturned milk crate, smoking a cigarette. Because Inez won't let him smoke inside the apartment, he's come up here. But dinner's almost ready now, so she's been sent to fetch him and bring him down, which she is more than happy to do. She'd wrangled an invitation to come for dinner on the third day of his visit, believing two days was time enough for the siblings to catch up. She'd arrived at the appointed time, but dinner was nowhere near ready—Inez was still washing the rice and soaking the beans, and the cilantro, garlic, onions, and peppers were all sitting out on the counter waiting to be turned into sofrito.

She'd been dying to meet this brother ever since she and Inez first became friends, ever since that first time Inez invited her over and she saw a picture of him in his soldier's uniform hanging on the living room wall. Inez had gestured to the picture and said, "That's my brother. He's pleased to meet you." But the man in the picture didn't seem as if anything ever had or ever could please him. His face was stern, his eyes belligerent. He hadn't looked anything like his kind, warmhearted sister. "When we're all together you can see it," Inez had said. "All the puzzle pieces clicking in." Downstairs in the apartment, she'd thought she could see past their starkly different complexions—Inez was pale where her brother was red, ruddy even—and detect their resemblance, but up here on the rooftop, sitting erect atop a milk crate as if he might be called on by a superior at any moment, Inez's brother looks like he isn't related to anyone but himself.

He turns when the door slams behind her, tensed as if for battle, but relaxes at the sight of her. Gallantly, he rises from the milk crate and offers it to her. She nods her thanks, thinking that in a family dominated by girls he must be used to giving way. All together there were four siblings, three sisters and one brother, who had come from Puerto Rico and had now spread across the Northeast. The other three had all gone to Connecticut. Only Inez had chosen to settle in New York. How was it that the older twin had picked Brooklyn, settling into this apartment in a brand-new housing development in Brownsville just a stone's throw away from the children's public library, while the other three opted for New England?

These were all things she could have asked her friend but had chosen not to. Now, on this rooftop whose heat shoots up through the thin soles of her borrowed sandals, she poses the questions to Inez's brother.

"She's not the older twin," he says. "And she didn't come here first."

"Why didn't she go to Connecticut?"

He shrugs and offers her his cigarette. When she declines, he flicks it over the edge of the rooftop. "She always wants to be different."

"That's what I want too." She hasn't meant to say such a thing out loud, especially not to a stranger, but as soon as she does, the truth of it shimmers through her. She knows why her friend would buck the trend. She, too, has a bevy of siblings, and though she loves them all it's hard to ever feel the separateness that she needs to define herself. Her brother is a Mason and two of her sisters became Eastern Stars like her mother, but she passed on joining even though it would have made her mother proud, even though it would have completed the set. Besides, he doesn't feel like a stranger to her. Her visits with his sister were all full of talk of him, the family's only boy. He's sandwiched between the twins and the baby girl—a middle child if you count Inez and her twin as one. He'd been drafted into the army, serving because he had to, not because he'd chosen to, and now that his time was done he'd come here to spend a week with his older sister. Soon enough he'd head back to the other two in New Haven.

"What's Inez's twin like?" she asks. "Is it hard to tell them apart?"

"They don't look like twins," he says. "They only look like sisters."

She wonders what he plans to do when he gets back to New Haven. He's twenty, like her, and she wonders if he's got his life figured out or if he's still searching. She wonders what he thinks of Brooklyn, a place where she has always lived and where she always expects to live. She wonders if he will stay in New Haven or go back to Puerto Rico, and then remembers Inez had said that their parents died some time ago. She thinks of the apartment buildings near Coney Island and how the people who live there can step over to the beach any time they like, whereas she and her family have to load a shopping cart full of towels and coolers and beach umbrellas and bump it down the subway station at Nostrand to take the A to Jay Street before switching to the F and how nice it would be if you could just grab a towel and walk out your door and be right there. She wonders if that is what it's like in Puerto Rico, if he could walk from his old home to the beach, if he could hear or see the ocean from wherever he stood. These are questions she could have easily asked his sister but had never thought to. Now, on the rooftop, facing the water tower on the adjacent roof, she burns with curiosity.

"You have to take a bus or drive—the ocean's not that close. Not close enough to see, but I can always hear it," he says. "Inez can't."

"Because she's been gone so long?"

"She never could," he says. It seems special, like a superpower, a rare gift, akin to the way her own brother can remember every word he's ever read. Before he got married and after he came home from the army, they'd spend the hour after church rolling loose change into paper wrappers to take to the bank, and he'd recite to her every article he'd read in that morning's paper so that listening to him had been like having her very own radio tuned to a station just for her. They hadn't owned a television yet, and even six months later when he bought one for their mother she was sure her brother was better than all those television shows combined.

He crouches beside her, his head close to her knee, to rummage through a small green sack that she hasn't noticed inches from her feet. "What's inside?" she asks. Never has she been so curious, but sitting on the rooftop on a summer night anything seems possible. There's no one to overhear her if she says something foolish. Anything she says can simply float to the night stars. She pretends that the ink-dark sky is the ocean and that she can swim it from here to his home.

"I'd like to take your picture." He pulls a compact black camera from his bag. A Brownie Hawkeye—her brother has one just like it. "If you give me your address, I'll send you a copy." He lines up the flasholder and attaches it to the camera's side. He holds the camera in both hands and aims it at her. "Ready?"

"Not like this?" she asks, meaning she's not dressed for picture-taking, meaning perhaps he should come back another day after she's visited the beauty parlor and had her hair washed, pressed, and curled, after she's powdered the sheen of sweat from her forehead, chin, and clavicle and switched her sundress for something less casual and far more lovely.

He releases the shutter, snapping a picture of her just as she is, sitting on the milk crate, before advancing the film to take another and another. He says, "Like this you are linda," and she can guess what the foreign word means. He pulls his jacket from the bag and turns it inside out before placing it on the rooftop's tarred floor. "Pretend you are on the beach and you are lying on a blanket."

He holds out his hand and she lowers herself onto his jacket. She leans back on her elbows and crosses one leg over the other, posing just the way she remembers Eartha Kitt posing for an issue of *Jet* the previous year. She pretends she is Eartha Kitt in a spangly evening gown rather than just herself clad in a cotton sundress with thick sturdy straps and shod in the thin-soled sandals she'd borrowed from her older sister without permission. She does as he suggests and pretends that she is on the beach, but she goes a step further. She pretends she is beautiful. She closes her eyes and pretends there is a breeze coming off the ocean they share and that the breeze is as soft and gentle as fingers ruffling the curls at her temples and ears. When she opens her eyes, the pretending is true and he's on the ground beside her, his hands lightly trailing through her hair, feathering across her cheek. When he looks at her, the sternness is gone and there is only longing. She feels like a breeze carried across the sea. She says,

"Your sister sent me up here to tell you dinner's almost ready," and lets him help her up. Standing, she brushes off her hands and feels grains of sand on her fingertips.

He apologizes for keeping them up here and away from their dinner. "After all," he says, "you must be hungry."

"Yes," she says, by which she means not at all. She can't imagine she will be hungry ever again.

Buen Provecho

We will never learn to speak Spanish—our mother fights us every step of the way. She wants nothing to do with her father's language, nothing that reminds her of him—including herself. We've seen the proof in the pictures, those Polaroids from the seventies capturing her attempts at being a foxy mama. She'd tried to transform her fine hair into an Afro, hoping the do would make the neighbors stop asking her what she was mixed with and put an end to the Puerto Ricans calling out to her on the street in a language she didn't speak. She'd heard that beer would kink her hair and lend it body, but all she'd ended up with were drunken curls.

Because we know the lengths to which she'll go, we keep our efforts secret and learn behind her back. On Saturdays we work on our weekly book reports at the Stone Avenue public library, and on our way home we stop to visit our grandfather's sister who lives in the projects nearby. Our titi buzzes us up, and when we get off on her floor she's standing in her doorway, waiting for us to get off the elevator, watching out to ensure we arrive in one piece.

She closes the door behind us and turns a series of locks

before sliding on the safety chain. Then she hugs us and says, "Come on in, kids. How are you?"

We hug back and respond, "No hablamos inglés," and our weekly game begins.

For the rest of our visit she'll speak only Spanish. It doesn't matter that we can't answer, let alone understand. We soak up her words, guess at their meanings, and do our best to follow along. After she sets the table, our titi tells us, "Sientense," and we take our seats. When she sets the food before us—arroz con pollo, arroz con gandules, arroz con jueyes, arroz con habichuelas, always arroz con something—we say gracias, and she pats our cheeks in approval. Before we take our first bites she says, "Buen provecho," and makes us repeat the same. We eat our fill of plates piled high with rice as our titi fills our ears with words. We remember please and thank you and I'm sorry and just a handful more— not enough to make a sentence, just enough to not offend. Our titi says these words are the bare necessities and that politeness will take us far. Just before we leave she bends and cries, "¡Besos! ¡Besos!" covers us in kisses, and makes us promise to come again soon. She wants us to give our mother her love, but of course our mother can't know that we were ever here.

We sling our book bags across our shoulders and troop out past the kids playing in the courtyard, past the teens leaning on the fences and checking their beepers, past the cars driving by with their booming systems, and past street after street of housing projects on the way to our own. We practice rolling our r's all the way home. "Arroz," we say, gagging at the back of our throats, struggling to master the trill. "Arroz. Arroz. Arroz." We sound like pirates—angry, gargling pirates—but we don't care. We only have ten blocks to practice. Once we turn up our street, we have to put our words away.

Still, they slip out when we're not careful. Hours after we've shown off our trove of borrowed books and our mother has checked our homework, she's at the sink straining the spaghetti for dinner when my brother points to my chair and whispers, "Sientate."

"Sientate," I whisper in response, pointing back at his. As if we've rehearsed it for a dance routine, we sit at the same time and scoot ourselves forward. Our mother joins us at the kitchen table, and we link hands and bow our heads and close our eyes to say grace. She squeezes our fingers at the end of the prayer to signal that we can eat. Taking up our forks, we twirl our spaghetti, forget ourselves, and say to each other, "Buen provecho."

Our mother's head snaps up. "What was that?" she asks. "What did you say?"

"Nothing," we lie.

"You know I don't like that kind of talk," she says. "I don't want to hear that in my house."

We hang our heads and squirm under her scrutiny, afraid to meet her eyes. She leaves her food untouched and watches us instead, eyes scanning back and forth between us as we sit quietly and do our best to pretend this whole thing never happened, until she suddenly pushes her plate away and rushes from the table.

If only we could say that we ran right after her, fast on her heels to apologize for the error of our ways. But even though our titi fed us only hours ago, we are hungry once again. Before we check on our mother, we finish our meals. After we've cleaned our plates, we polish off hers.

Once we've eaten everything in sight, we seek her out and find her in her bedroom curled into a ball on top of the comforter, her back to the light shining in from the hallway. We didn't mean to make her cry.

"We're sorry, Ma," we call from the doorway. "We didn't mean the words we said."

She flinches when she hears our voices, covers her hands with her ears, and curls her body even tighter. "I just don't want to hear that."

We leave our words behind as we kick off our shoes and climb onto her bed and pry our mother apart. We each take a side and surround her, close as mercy, as we uncurl her legs and burrow beneath her arms. We soothe her into silence, patting her shoulders and back to beg pardon, huddling close to make her hush. Drowsy with dinner and the warmth of our mother, we sleep glued to her all night. In the morning, she'll forgive us and we will put this all behind us. We'll never speak of this night again. No, we will never say another word.

Quarter Rican

More like a Quarter Rican," Tio Chalí said. I was fourteen that summer and my uncle was twenty-three. Two weeks earlier, I'd boarded a plane at JFK for Puerto Rico. It was the third summer in a row that my folks had sent me over to visit my grandfather's family, and the first time I'd made the trip by myself, unaccompanied by Titi Inez. At fourteen, I was finally old enough to get my working papers, and I'd wanted to stay at home in Brooklyn to have my first summer job. Most of my friends had found jobs in rec centers and fast-food joints. My best friend had taken a job at the McDonald's on Atlantic Avenue—she'd have given me free milkshakes and hot apple pies all summer long. Me? I'd hoped to run the P.O.P. ticket booth at Coney Island's Astroland Park or to work the concession stand and make popcorn at the Metropolitan or Duffield movie theaters. Instead I had to spend the summer tucked away on an island, stuck in my grandfather's house, while my friends at home made money hand over fist.

Last summer, Chalí had been as trapped as me. Hungry for a place to deejay, he'd tried every spot to see if someone would take him on, but no one would. This summer he had more gigs than he could handle. He disappeared every night and napped

away the mornings, coming out of his room for breakfast in midafternoon. I was keeping him company at the kitchen table while
Abuela made him something to eat. When I'd arrived two weeks
ago, they'd all exclaimed over how tall I'd gotten. My grandfather
had positioned me beside Abuela for comparison. The summers
before, she and I had been the same height, but now I easily towered over his tiny wife. That night when Titi Cristina came home
from work I towered over her too. Every day since I'd arrived
Chalí had made some comment, telling me I was a palm tree,
saying I should play basketball. He said that I must have gotten
the height from the black side of my family. "But I'm also Puerto
Rican," I'd said. "It could have also come from there."

That's when he'd called me Quarter Rican. My uncle plucked
four quarters from the pocket of his jeans and plunked them
down on the kitchen table. "That's me," he said, lining up the
quarters near the bottle of syrup. "One two three four." Then he
slid one quarter away from the others and over to me. "And this
one, nena, is you."

Abuela turned from the stove in time to see what he had done.
With her free hand, she pinched him. "Chalí, leave Nadia alone!"
She upturned the frying pan and dumped a pan-sized pancake—
the biggest pancake I'd ever seen—onto his plate.

My uncle didn't notice how his words stung. He poured syrup
over his mega-pancake and devoured it while I sat across from
him, a throbbing, living welt. If I'd complained, he'd have been
bewildered. What he'd said was supposed to be a joke between
us, something I was supposed to find as funny as he did.

"It's important," my mother had said when I'd complained
about the visit. "You need to know your family." Tío Chalí's
father was my grandfather, but his mother was not my grandmother. She was my grandfather's second wife; *Abuela* was

simply a courtesy title. Chalí and I weren't all the way family. Just half of my mother was his sister. Part of my uncle's blood was my blood, but only one quarter's worth, not enough to make me anything more than a summer vacation relative.

After he finished his breakfast, Chalí sent me outside with those quarters to the bochinchera's house with orders to bring us back two limbers. When I scooped up the quarters, they weighed down my shorts, making it difficult for me to lift my legs, forcing me to limp.

When I returned, Abuela was in her bedroom watching tele-novelas and Chalí was gone from the table. I followed the muffled sound of music down the hall to my uncle's room and knocked. Inside, there was barely any space for another body, so crowded was the room with his equipment. Chalí's bed was pushed into a corner and crates full of LPs topped his nightstand, blotted out the mirror on his bureau, and took up all the space on the floor. Each night he lugged these crates out to the car, piling them in the trunk of the family's dusty green station wagon, ready to spin the night away at the clubs.

He didn't take the limber I handed him. "Later," he said. "Nadia, check this out." I joined him behind his makeshift dee-jay stand. I squeezed the plastic cup that held my coco limber, pushed up the icy treat to my waiting mouth, licking the cold sweet slushy dessert while my uncle spun his tunes.

He played the season's hits—"Poison," "Bonita Applebum," and "The Humpty Dance"—seamlessly blending one song into the other. I closed my eyes and I was back in Brooklyn, lying on my stomach on the floor in my living room, listening to the radio, my head close to the speaker as I tuned in to 98.7 KISS FM.

I opened my eyes and Chalí shook his head. "I can't believe you got so tall," he said. He piled his hands atop my head and pushed down like a game show contestant pressing a buzzer, pretending to stunt my growth. "One day," he predicted, "you might be as tall as me. Height runs in our family."

"But I'm only a Quarter Rican," I reminded him.

"No, nena," he said, "that's not true at all."

Rerun

I f we flip the channels fast enough, we can turn almost anyone Puerto Rican, blurring black and white into Boricua. When we can't find a good show with a Puerto Rican actor, we make our own, turning the knob selector on the TV as hard and fast as we can, watching all the brown faces click by until our mother yells from the kitchen for us to choose a show and stick to it.

Reruns all summer long because cable is brand-new and only for the rich. Like everyone else we want our MTV, but we never get it. We're stuck with the same old summer vacation lineup of mornings filled with game shows and soap operas, of summer syndication afternoons and reruns of *Fantasy Island, Gidget, Good Times, Happy Days,* and *Trapper John, M.D.* Our mother says it's important to see oneself on the big and little screens; she goes on and on about growing up watching Rita Moreno in *West Side Story* and Nichelle Nichols on *Star Trek,* and every Easter she makes us sit through *The Greatest Story Ever Told* to see José Ferrer play Herod the Roman tetrarch.

Satisfying our black side is easy enough. We've got George and Weezy, Fred and Lamont Sanford. We've got Webster, Tootie, Arnold, and Willis. We've got Raj, Dwayne, Rerun, and Dee. We've got the Evans family—Florida, James, Michael, Thelma, and J.J. a.k.a. Kid Dy-no-mite—but we have to work to find the Boricuas. We collect Puerto Rican actors the way other kids collect comics, valued all the more because they're so rare. The Boricuas are hard to find and easy to miss. Cast to blend in, they play Asians, Italians, Jews, Mexicans, and Romans—almost anything but themselves. Sure, we know we can find plenty on channels 41 and 47, on Univision and Telemundo, where all the shows are in Spanish, but that's a language neither one of us speaks.

"Don't give up," I tell my sister, who's taking her turn at turning.

We sift through reruns of old shows, hoping for Antonio Fargas on *Starsky & Hutch* or Erik Estrada on *CHiPs*. We can usually glimpse Gregory Sierra on *Sanford and Son* or *Barney Miller*. Last week we found him on *All in the Family*, playing a militant Jew who gets blown up by a car bomb the moment he steps out of Archie Bunker's house. The men are easier to find than the women—unless you count Maria on *Sesame Street*, but we're too old for shows that are meant for babies.

What we really want is Irene Cara in *Fame* or Charo on *The Love Boat*, but my sister lands on *The Electric Company* and we get Rita Moreno instead. We don't want the woman our mother grew up watching, but she's everywhere we turn. She's the Siamese concubine Tuptim in the *King and I*, she's the cleaning lady on *The Cosby Show* who works in the hospital where Dr. Huxtable delivers all the babies, and she's here on PBS all summer long. But we don't need a new abuela. We buried our grandmother two years ago and there's no going back.

It's too soon to settle, so we keep playing channel roulette. Finding Boricuas requires a careful hand and a discerning eye.

We cross our fingers and hope for someone good. "It's all in the wrist," I say, determined to do better with my turn at the knob.

"Stop here!" my sister says when we hear the theme song to *The Love Boat*. I step back in time to see Charo's face encircled by the life preserver. "Titi Charo!" my sister whispers, happy with the day's find.

We've seen Charo on more episodes of *The Love Boat* than we can count, and we like to pretend that she is our famous, flamboyant aunt. She plays a Mexican woman, Angelina Patricia Ruiz Inez Lopez, or "April" Lopez, who returns to the *Pacific Princess* again and again, morphing from stowaway to singer to language tutor to nanny. There's the one where she's hired as the ship's entertainment to sing during dinner but she really wants to be a cruise director. At night she performs in a slinky silver off-the-shoulder dress with a thigh-high slit and layers of fringe, and during the day she shadows Julie McCoy to learn the ropes of cruise directing and ruins bingo and shuffleboard in the process. Then there's the one where Gopher falls asleep while watching an old movie and dreams that it's the 1940s and the *Pacific Princess* is carrying soldiers to France for war, and Charo plays a Brazilian spy and double agent. Today's is the one where she's a stowaway seeking a career in show business. Dressed in a white peasant blouse and a long red flouncy skirt, she's all big hair, big lips, big accent, and big personality. She boards the ship with an armful of souvenirs, floppy hats, and sombreros to sell, but when Gopher turns his back she runs and hides in the housekeeper's closet. We lie on our stomachs, stretched out in front of the TV on the floor in our living room, and watch, rapt, as Captain Stubing, Julie, and the housekeeper discover her in the laundry cart, buried beneath a pile of the ship's bedsheets.

Though she looks nothing like either our aunt or our mother, that doesn't stop us from believing we could be related—Puerto Ricans come in all colors and shades. We clamor to claim her as kin. If Titi Charo came over to watch us, we'd be sure to have fun. There would be music and dancing and cuchi-cuchi. We'd trade her for our real aunt any day, swapping out the titi who threatens us with her chancletas, who only leaves her apartment twice a month, on the first and fifteenth to pick up her check, and whose adult son still lives with her because he's too lazy to find a place of his own. We'd prefer a titi like Charo who actually liked us, who didn't mind the way we looked, who didn't complain that we get darker and darker every year. Instead of teaching us to play the guitar and sing, our real titi sucks away our summer break, convincing our mother to bring us inside every day from noon to one when she says the sun is highest in the sky. She tells our mother this will protect us from the hole in the ozone but warns us that we'll never find husbands and that no one will ever want us if we turn into negritas. Whenever she comes over to watch us, she ridicules our hair, calling us mini Stevie Wonders. She pulls the beads and the foil from the tips of our braids, unravels our cornrows all the way to our scalps, and presses our hair straight and flat with her hot comb. She pops us with her chancleta any time we fidget, pinches our cheeks, and warns us that we'll have to be smart because we'll never be beautiful. This is not a thing Titi Charo would ever stoop to say.

After Captain Stubing puts her off in Mazatlán, Titi Charo/April Lopez sneaks back on again and convinces Julie to let her sing. Free of her flounces and dressed in a strapless lace-topped black evening gown, she sits on a stool and leads the band in a song that shows off her guitar skills before leaping to her feet, undulating like a belly dancer, and shimmying around the dance floor, charming all of the passengers with cuchi-cuchi effervescence.

The phone rings and our mother yells for us to turn down the TV. She plucks the receiver from the cradle and can't get a word in for a full five minutes, so we know she's talking to our aunt.

"No, they ran away this morning," she says. "I woke up and they were gone. No note. Not a clue. Since I finally got some time to myself I'm watching soap operas." We flip over and stare when we hear the fib. Our mother looks over the kitchen counter and winks. She laughs and says, "Of course I'm joking!" and we snicker to think our aunt could be so gullible. "The twins are right here, they're watching TV. *Love Boat*. An episode with Charo. No, not Chano. *Charo*. Yes you do. Sure you remember. She sang on Merv Griffin, and we used to watch her on Ed Sullivan. You know, the guitarrista? Yes, that's right. The white woman from Spain."

Making a Way

Two weeks and a day after Bobby Kennedy's assassination you take the kids to see your husband's sister, their closest relative on their father's side. Once a month you bring them to Inez—your way of making sure they don't forget their heritage. Five years ago, your husband convinced you to move to New Haven so he could live closer to his other two sisters. You let him take you away from the neighborhood where you had lived your entire life, away from your own sisters and brother and mother, and away from the one sister of his that you genuinely like. Two years into your new life, an altercation with a neighbor that turned bloody sent him fleeing back to Puerto Rico to escape arrest. Though he promised to return once things cooled down on the block, a year passed without word. You found yourself stranded with three young children in a strange city, with mounting expenses and two sisters-in-law who were no help at all. Your mother and siblings bailed you out, scraping together enough money to bring you and the children back to Brooklyn, where you learned from Inez that your husband was alive and well on the island and had no plans of returning any time soon.

Like always, Inez greets the children in Spanish and smothers them in kisses, but instead of keeping them near this time, she sends them into the living room, tells them to be gentle with her record albums, and warns them not to interrupt the adults, who need to talk. You join her in the kitchen and take a seat at her table, choosing the one near the open window. Here in this apartment on the eighth floor of the Van Dyke Houses in Brownsville is where it all began. Here on a wall above the couch in Inez's living room is where you first saw the picture of the man that you would marry. Here on the rooftop of Inez's building is where you first met that man. And here you come routinely, now that he's left you, to keep his memory alive for his children, who are forgetting him, to receive news from Inez because he's long since stopped communicating with you, and to remind yourself that it—the love, the courtship, the marriage—really did take place. It is all such a tangle, and Inez is the human tether between you and your husband. For all that's happened between your two families, she is still your best friend. With her there is no awkwardness, no blame. There is no taking sides—there are no sides to take. There is only a life to make with the skeins of all these unraveling threads.

Inez pulls a pack of Winstons from the pocket of her pedal pushers, shakes out a cigarette, and tells you of her plans to spend a month in Puerto Rico this summer. Her brother—your husband—would like her to bring the kids along for a visit. This is the first time he's asked to see the children since he's been gone. You would prefer that he come back and see them for himself, come back and be their father and your husband, but you convince yourself that this, at last, is progress.

Inez hands you two airline tickets, whose blue paper jackets read PAN AMERICAN AIRWAYS SYSTEMS in large blue letters across the center white stripe and, below, in smaller white

letters, ISSUED BY PAN AMERICAN WORLD AIRWAYS
INC. WORLD'S MOST EXPERIENCED AIRLINE. MEMBER
OF INTERNATIONAL AIR TRANSPORT ASSOCIATION.
Inside each jacket is a ticket for a round-trip flight from John
F. Kennedy International Airport to Isla Verde International
Airport. You wait for the third ticket, but Inez drops into a chair
and lights her cigarette.

"Where's the other one?"

"Just the two," Inez says.

Clearly, there has been some mistake. "What does this mean?
He wants me to pick who gets to go? How can I possibly—"

Inez cuts you off. "He's only sending for the boys."

You pluck the cigarette from Inez's hand and take a long drag.
You have no words. Thankfully, the kids are in the other room,
too absorbed in pawing through Inez's albums and fighting over
which songs to play to overhear what their father has done.
Thankfully, you have this cigarette to calm your nerves and give
your hands something to do. "I don't believe this."

Inez says, "You know how he is."

Do you?

What you know is that you married a man who can abandon
his family without qualm, a man who can put his wife and children out of his mind with ease. Somehow, you'd gotten used to his
callousness, his indifference, his insensitivity when it came to you,
but this new trick of sending two tickets when you have three children, of skipping over and leaving out your daughter, is a brand-
new low. What you know is that it's a Friday afternoon in late June,
the first official day of summer, and it's noisier outside than yester-
day because now—everywhere, all over—kids are out of school.
What you know is that it is June 21, 1968, and Martin and Bobby
have both been killed and your marriage is now truly over. The

events are not related, but you'll never stop putting them together, never stop associating the end of the two civil rights leaders' lives with the end of your marriage. You're not a protester and you've never sat down at a lunch counter when a sign said you couldn't. You've never had to integrate anything, and for as long as you can remember you've always been able to go wherever you've wanted. Perhaps a marriage isn't much when compared to a string of assassinations—first Medgar and John, then Malcolm, now Martin and Bobby—yet it is still the end of something possible, the end of a possible way of being, and your marriage is just the latest thing to die during this decade that has become a season for killing things.

You hand back the cigarette and pick up the two airline tickets once more. In each palm you balance a ticket light as a feather, light as the straw that breaks the camel's back.

"How long until you leave?"

Inez says, "Five weeks."

"I want all three to go."

"There's no money for her ticket," Inez reminds you.

"I'll get the money," you promise.

"How?"

"I'll find a way."

"But there is no way." Inez knows he's never sent you any money. She knows just how little you have to live on.

"I'll make a way out of no way," you decide, echoing a refrain from your childhood, channeling your mother's voice. Every morning she lined up the children, looking you and your siblings over before you left for school, giving you each a spoonful of cod-liver oil to keep sickness at bay, and calling down prayers upon your head, beseeching the Lord to make a way out of no way and keep all her children safe and sound and fed and warm. And, somehow, you all were. Somehow, she did. How she fed and raised six young children on a widow's pension you never knew, and she never said. All you know is that, somehow, she made a way out of no way and now it falls to you to do the same.

It is easier said than done. More than prayers are needed to create money from thin air. You refuse to ask your mother and siblings—they have already given so much. You think to save money by slashing the grocery budget. You stop buying soda and brew pitchers of iced tea instead. At Pathmark, you buy no-frills canned vegetables instead of Del Monte and Green Giant. You make meat loaf until you are sick of it. No more money for the ice cream truck. No more trips to the candy store. No more treats. You scrimp and scrimp and scrimp and still there is not enough money. Saving takes you only so far. You gamble with the siphoned dollars. You send the kids to the roller rink on Empire Boulevard and spend full days at the bingo hall with your mother, where you never win. You play the numbers; you play every number you can think of. First your own birthday, then your children's, then your mother's, your brother's, all your sisters' birthdays, and then every other relative's birthday you can remember. You play Inez's. You even play your husband's. You play whole numbers, day numbers and night numbers. You play the numbers singly and in bolitas, straight and in all possible combinations. You borrow a dream book and sleep with a notepad by your bedside. You chase your dreams upon waking, trying to capture them before they wisp away so you can look them up in the book and play their corresponding numbers. Susceptible to the last thing you watch on TV before bed, Don Adams, Carol Burnett, Barbara Eden, Sally Field, Martin Landau, Dean Martin, Elizabeth Montgomery, Roger Moore, Greg Morris,

Nichelle Nichols, Marlo Thomas, and Lawrence Welk parade through your dreams all night, leaving you with nothing to play.

Too often, you consider letting those two airline tickets go to waste and serving your husband a keen rough justice. Now that you're back in Brooklyn, the children are surrounded by family. Your mother and sister live one flight up the stairs in the same building. Your baby sister is a mere six blocks away. Your mother's cousins live two blocks over. And, too, there is Inez. Don't the children have all the family they need? But there is more than blood to consider. There is an inheritance, another entire language inside their heads waiting to be awakened, a language lying dead upon their tongues that you cannot call to life. This is what you want for them—to be all the pieces of themselves. They have the chance to see their father's homeland with their own eyes, to go to a place you've never been, a place you cannot go, a place you— who have lived in only three locales—cannot even fathom. Until your husband, you'd never lived anywhere but Brooklyn. The first and only time you'd ever been on a plane was when you flew to Oklahoma to live with him on the base where he was stationed. The only other trip you'd taken was the one mini cruise with your mother and her Eastern Star sisters, where you sailed to Trinidad and Tobago, though you couldn't tell the difference between the two, and you brought back an oversized wooden spoon and fork to hang in your kitchen as proof that you had been to an island, that you had crossed a body of water and touched another shore. How you thought those trips would change you and be harbingers of new places to see and of better days to come.

On a night when you're too tired for television, you dream that you are riding the subway. You're on an unfamiliar train—not the A. It's not one of the old Thunderbirds you know but one of the brand-new trains. There are no fans in the ceiling, and air conditioning pimples your flesh. Instead of a two-seater, you're sitting in a long row. A woman sits between you and the handrail; the seat on your other side is empty. A man, unkempt and shaggy, scolds you for taking up two spaces and says you need to choose a seat. He wedges himself between you and the woman, pushing you over into the empty seat. You shout at him. Now the two of you are standing, facing each other, and yelling. Somehow, you have grown taller so that you are both the same height, and you can look him in the eye. This close to his face, he does not look unkempt but handsome. You are livid that he's pushed you over and taken your seat, and you refuse to back down. You both keep yelling as you stand in front of the now abandoned seats. In his anger he grabs your arms, and his fingers dig into the flesh just above your elbows. You are standing so close that as he yells his lips brush yours. You wake up feeling chastened, oddly disturbed, still caught in the grip of strange hands.

You don't imagine this scenario will be found in any book.

The next morning you're washing the breakfast dishes, soaking a saucepot in hot soapy water to loosen the caked-on oatmeal. Though it's summer, you've taken away your children's favorite breakfast cereals to further economize. Gone are the boxes with mascots of colorful roosters, tigers, toucans, and white rabbits. Now a white-haired man in a wideawake hat and cravat looks back from a canister of old-fashioned oats—the latest, newest change. So much has changed within the past five years, the least of which is your marriage. Five years ago, your husband packed a car and drove the family from Brooklyn to New Haven and now you are back home again, your own round-trip journey. Five years ago, everyone called the airport your children will fly out of Idlewild, although it had a different official name because the president was still then living. Five years ago, Medgar Evers, John Kennedy, Malcolm X, Martin Luther King, and Bobby Kennedy were all still living, breathing men. Five years ago, you could not comprehend how uncertain was the future, or how drastically the world would change.

You scrub the saucepot and rinse it clean. Under the stream of hot water your wedding ring gleams dully on your finger, tarnished from years of dishwashing, sheened with a film left by lotion and soap residue. You don't know why you're still wearing it. He hasn't really been your husband in years—not since the moment he left.

Days later you call Inez to tell her you've hit the number and have the money for the third ticket.

Inez is all happiness and curiosity. "What did you play?" she wants to know.

"Seven sixty-nine," you tell her, which, really, she should have been able to guess. Everyone knows that it's the number to play for things that, like your marriage, are now dead.

What the Mouth Knows

We search the face of every old Puerto Rican man we meet, hoping to see our grandfather's face looking back at us. The way to and from school is paved with old brown Boricua men. Up Riverdale and Rockaway, over on Thatford, Osborne, or Watkins, down on Newport or Lott Avenues, they sit outside raggedy shops, rocking back on rickety milk crates, smoking, and listening to small radios at their feet blaring news in rapid-fire Spanish. They carry out folding chairs and plop down to whittle, bringing out knives and blocks of wood to carve little frogs with wide, wondering eyes. They yell in Spanish at everyone passing by, calling out to the morning workers on their way to the train and bus stops, to the men heading for the liquor store in the bright light of the day, to the women out to buy groceries at Key Food, and to all the kids who've turned the empty and abandoned lot at the corner junction into a place to play.

We're too slick to let them catch us as we take our fill of looking. We slow down and retie our laces, or we wait for the light to turn before crossing, just to buy ourselves the time to check them out. Less than neighbors and more than strangers, the old

Boricuas intrigue us as they yell at all the passersby in a language we feel that we should know.

We never answer, even when we hear "¡Mira!" which sounds almost just like my name. Even if we knew the language, we don't dare talk to strangers. We know better. We know there are adults who like to snatch up kids and adults who hide razors in Halloween candy. We know how often kids go missing and end up with their faces plastered on milk cartons. We know people find newborn babies in dumpsters every single day. We know where we are from. We know where we live. We watch our would-be grandfathers, but we don't ever get too close.

Because we've never seen our grandfather's face, every old Boricua becomes a possibility. He could walk right by us and we would never even know. Our mother claims to have no pictures. When pestered, she asks, "Why in the world would I want to see his face?" But we would like to see it, to see if in her father's face there are any hints of us.

With nothing to go by, any old man we see could be our grandfather come back from Puerto Rico to spy on us, to let us know he's watching us on the sly, that he's found a way to be near us without upsetting our mother. He knows she's never forgiven him for leaving, so he lies in wait to watch us pass each day on our way to and from school. We want to believe that he is simply biding his time, waiting for the right moment to reveal his presence, to tell us that he never left, that he has loved us all along, that he has always been here, nearby, and that this was as close as he could get without giving away the secret. Maybe we're old enough to know better and maybe—deep inside—we do, but this fantasy sustains us until we outgrow our craving for his love.

We are hoping for a signal, some way to know which old man

is the one we want. We need a way to identify him, to sort him from the possibles before we can bring him home, reconcile him and our mother, and become the family we never were but always could have been. We devise ways to give him a nudge, to let him know that we know and that it's okay to come out of hiding. My brother, who has been watching too much *A-Team*, suggests kidnapping. "Let's nab one," he says. "I bet we can find ways to make him talk."

Four blocks from home, we cross at the corner and I point out the man who works the repair lot. "What about that one?"

Sandwiched between two abandoned buildings is his lot with its orange-and-green corrugated fencing, behind which rubber car tires are stacked high, old cars and vans with shattered windshields and flat tires are idle, and broken bicycles with dented frames and bent and missing wheels are tilted drunkenly against each other.

As we near this old man, who is the only living thing on this dead, dead street, who sits outside in front of his handmade *Flats Fixed* sign, listening to the radio and repairing a broken bike, my brother whispers, "Maybe," before stepping on my laces to pull them loose.

I kneel to fix them, buying us time for a longer look. There is possibility in his watchfulness, in the way he sits still as a spy, his body rooted to the spot, while his hands glide from handlebar to stem of the broken bicycle, moving with the same tenderness our mother uses to comb my hair.

I loop my laces into a bow and pull tight, and when I look up the old man is looking right back at me. His thumb trips the lever and rings the broken bike's shining silver bell. He laughs, revealing a terrible mouth, a maw of crooked and rotting teeth. "Ha ha, I scared you, nena!" He rings the bell again and grips the handlebars as if he's about to speed off into the sunset. "Vroom, nena!" He rings the bell again. "Come in!" he cackles. And again. "Sorry, nobody home!"

"Come on." My brother yanks me to my feet. "He's crazy as a loon!"

The sound of the old man's bell follows us as we take off running. We race those whole four blocks, running all the way home, chased by his laughter, as something more than language dies upon our tongues.

We Ask Why

Come summer we're getting packed up and shipped out, sent off to Puerto Rico where our father is from and where he has long been living, ever since he left us. We haven't seen our father in years—we have no desire to see him now. We ask our mother why we have to go and give up our fast-approaching summer. We ask why she can't just leave well enough alone.

We've already made our summer plans. We've aired out our swim trunks, bathing suits, and shower shoes. We're ready for horseplay at the nearby public pool, for holding our breath underwater, for playing Marco Polo, for trying to dunk every kid we see. We're ready for the deep end of the pool.

"This is better than the pool," she says, setting out our after-school snack. "You'll have beaches instead. There's nothing but beaches there."

We ask, "Can't we just go to Coney Island or Rockaway Beach instead?"

She says, "We're never going back there." Last summer, those beaches were overrun by medical waste, polluted with hypodermic needles and syringes that had washed ashore. We were used to the occasional baby diaper floating by as we played in the water, but needles filled with AIDS were where our mother drew the line. "The beaches where you're going will be clean."

We ask her how she knows if she's never been.

All she says is, "Trust me."

But how can we trust her after she's pulled this dirty trick of waiting until our summer vacation was close enough to taste and then dropping this surprise upon us? We were hoping this would be the summer we'd be tall enough to ride the Cyclone in Astroland Park, but instead of speeding down the curves, loops, and turns of the wooden roller coaster, we'll be going to LaGuardia to fly to a place we've never been, to see a man we convince ourselves we don't even miss.

We push away our plates and try to change her mind.

We tell her, "We'll be bored."

She says, "I can't make either one of you interesting."

We tell her we'll be lonely.

She says, "You'll have each other."

We say, "That's not enough. We'll miss hanging out with other kids. We don't want to leave our friends."

She says, "There will be plenty of kids. You'll get to meet your other brothers and sisters."

We ask, "How many?"

She says, "Four so far. At least as far as I know." She says, "Your father doesn't waste time."

She leaves us in the kitchen with our questions and heads off to her room. We follow and watch as she pulls down the suitcase from the top of her bedroom closet and carries it down the hallway and into our room. We linger in our doorway as she starts to pack our bag. From the bottom of our closet, she pulls our sneakers, sandals, and jellies. From our lower drawers she takes our T-shirts and denim shorts. From the upper drawers she pulls our undershirts, underwear, and folded socks. She packs like she means business.

We ask if we really have to go.

She says, "The tickets are already paid for," and we know what that means.

We ask why she is doing this to us. "We don't even know him," we say.

She says, "Of course you do," and balls eight pairs of our socks, tosses them into the belly of the suitcase, changes her mind, and takes them back out.

We knew him once—when we were babies, when we were toddlers, when he was simply there and we didn't know that time with him would wisp into memory. We do not remember his face. We cannot recall his touch, his kiss, his voice. We have no memories of his love. All we know is that we'll be flying alone together wearing tags around our necks so the flight attendants know to keep an eye on us as we unaccompanied minors accompany each other to see our father because our mother wants us to have a relationship with him even though she couldn't.

We ask why she chose him in the first place. We ask her why they married. We ask if they were in love.

"I was," she says. "I think he was too. For a time anyway."

We ask her what went wrong. "Too many things," she says. "For starters, I thought he was black. Technically he is, but it's not the same. There are many shades of black and he was a different shade from me." He was black, she says, but not African American. Black from an island. Black with splashes of Spaniard and hints of Taíno. Black in a way he could ignore when he chose. Black in a way that misled her into thinking they could make it a go but kept him looking at his wife and children as if they were strangers. Black in a way that was not binding, that could not bind him to us and make him stay.

She snaps our suitcase closed and tells us what it's like to compete with an island, to love a man with oceans in his eyes and the horizon in his heart. She says, "You just can't win."

"We hate him," we say.

She says, "He won't care."

We say, "We won't go."

She says, "That's what you think."

We ask, "Who'll look after us?"

She says he won't let us come to any harm while we are in his care.

We ask her who will kiss us good night.

She laughs. "It certainly won't be him."

We ask her if he'll feed us.

She says, "He's not going to let you starve."

We ask her if he'll love us.

She says, "How could I possibly know?"

That Island

My husband is also from that island, she tells the new neighbor, meaning Puerto Rico, but after the other woman has said it, she doesn't dare repeat it, not now that she knows how wrong she's pronounced it all these years. *Porta Rico* she's always said. Her husband had never corrected her. Which part, her new neighbor asks, rattling off names— San Juan? Bayamón? Río Piedras? Caguas? Ponce?—but she has no idea.

Her new neighbor sets two kitchen chairs in front of the living room window and invites her to sit. The new neighbor isn't new at all, only new to her; *she's* the one who's recently moved in. She's always lived in Brooklyn but never before in housing projects, so while her neighbor sets out a green tin of soda crackers and boils water for coffee, she peers through the window's metal bars right out onto the street, the cracked sidewalk, the dinged cars, and out across Pitkin Avenue to the row of stores—the bodega, the Chinese restaurant, the barbershop, the dollar store, and the video rental place—all teeming with people. Her own living room window looks out onto a stone courtyard where she hopes her baby granddaughter can one day play. "You don't look old enough to be an abuela," her neighbor says, and she's not—only forty-six—but age isn't always measured in years.

Calling it *that island* makes it sound as if she holds a grudge against the place, blaming a landmass in the middle of the ocean rather than the man himself for the problem that was their marriage. The truth is that she knows next to nothing about that island, except that it's where he's from, where he runs away to when he abandons her and their three children, and where he marries the new woman even though he's not yet divorced. She knows that island is a place where things disappear—husbands, love, and marriage. All that ever returns are her three children, whom she dutifully hands over every June, trying not to complain but to smile and be grateful that he still wants to see them even though he only ever sends airfare for the two boys and she has to play numbers and beg her mother and sisters for help to send the girl too.

But this is all so long ago. Her children are adults now; they've made peace with it all. She thought she had too, but just hearing her new neighbor introduce herself and say that she and her family are from Puerto Rico disturbs that long ago hard-earned peace, reminding her how that marriage of hers had been doomed from the start. For how could she love a man she never really knew, and how could she have ever known him when she couldn't even correctly pronounce the place from which he'd come?

What the Tide Returns

She counts the children as they come through the door—one, two, and three—to reassure herself that they are hers. She can't say just how happy she is to see them; she's missed them all summer long. She hardly recognizes them; they're browner than ever before and somehow warmer to the touch. She hugs them and her hands come away coated with fine grains of sand.

Both boys come back taller and sporting fresh haircuts. The girl is fuller around the hips and her hair is braided in a different style. All three come back with more clothes than when they left. They return with an extra suitcase stuffed full of shorts, tees, and swimsuits she never bought them, in colors, patterns, and prints she never knew they liked.

They've spent the summer in Puerto Rico, staying with their father and his new wife, and they have now returned to Brooklyn as strangers. They are the not the kids she sent to the island, not the children she put on the plane, but they are what the tide returns. She can feel the difference in their sun-warmed skin. All summer they've slept in a house and, now that they know the difference, her little apartment is no longer enough. She can read the truth in their ocean-filled eyes—now they know they are poor. They've traded in a summer of riding the subway for being ferried in their father's car; they've swapped playing in the public pool for basking on the beach. At dinner that night they tell stories of knocking mangoes off trees, of their father taking a machete to a coconut, and of them drinking coconut water straight from the gourd. They tell her that the coconuts in Puerto Rico look nothing like the ones in the cartoons resembling hairy bowling balls and that instead they are large, smooth, and green. Now they know things like this, details she can hardly imagine.

And isn't this what she wanted? For them to spend quality time with their father and get to know his culture, to know that it was also theirs, to not have to choose which side of themselves to nourish while the other side withered?

She waits for them to become hers again, yet even after they've been home for hours, they don't revert to the children she remembers. All afternoon and evening they wander the apartment disoriented, using words she doesn't recognize to ask for things she doesn't have. Now, instead of Mom or Ma, they all call her Mami. They've carried the island back with them, and around them it shimmers, hovering—she can sense its invisible, tangible pull. But no matter who they've become, they spare her their summer stack of Polaroids, so she doesn't have to see their father's new life without her. On their way off to bed, they file into her room and tell her how they've missed her, how happy they are to be back. They shower her with kisses and she feels their kisses drying, like salt water, on her cheek.

Feliz Navidad

On Christmas we wake up Puerto Rican. That's when our grandmother stops pretending that hers is our only blood and lets our grandfather's bleed back in. She stands at the feet of our beds and pulls on our blanketed toes. "Wake up, you two," she says, holding up an album cover. "Merry Christmas."

All year long she hides the José Feliciano album from us, but, like magic, it appears on Christmas morning. While all the other families in our building are listening to Nat King Cole, Donny Hathaway, and the Temptations, we'll be jamming to a blind Puerto Rican guitarist.

Bodies warm from our beds, hair mussed from our pillows, and eyes crusty from our good deep sleeps, we follow our grandmother down the hall. As we stumble along in our footed G.I. Joe and She-Ra pajamas, she leads us into the living room and straight to the record player on the end table. She lifts the dust cover, slides the record from its sleeve, sets it on the turntable, and lowers the needle. "Knock yourselves out," she says, abandoning us for the kitchen.

This is her only present to us. Today she doesn't mind that we are not just hers but our grandfather's as well. Today we're allowed to be not only African American but also Puerto Rican, to be all the parts of ourselves. Today we can play our record as many times as we want, as loud as we like, until our mother comes home, dead tired from her overtime shift. When she gets here, we'll tear bows and shiny wrapping paper off the Jem, Voltron, Transformers, and Teddy Ruxpin toys we asked for. Then she'll stagger off to bed and we'll have to keep quiet. For now, we're allowed to play our music and make noise.

We want just this one thing for Christmas—to play this record that draws us closer to our grandfather. He left New York for Puerto Rico when his kids were little, before we grandkids ever existed. He's never been back to Brooklyn to see us. He's a ghost of a man, flimsier than the tinsel we drape from the artificial branches of our artificial tree, a shining sliver of a thin, thin thread. This record is as close to him as we can get, a tether to pull him near. We can't compete with an island, and we are not Christmas-card cute. We're rough from playing in the streets, strong and wiry from swinging on monkey bars and climbing the stone animals in the courtyard of our housing projects, nimble from setting off Roman candles, jumping jacks, moon whistlers, and skyrockets fast enough that our fingers don't get scorched. Our knees are skinned from playing skelly and shooting marbles, our elbows and arms scabbed from fighting like we mean it. We're nothing to write home about, yet our mother writes to her father several times a year, sending letters across the ocean to update him on our progress, mailing him school pictures so he can see us for himself. We never hear back. We've long since stopped hoping for visits, for birthday or Christmas cards. A simple phone call on a day like today would do. We'd love to hear his voice.

Instead we hear the cuatro, the güiro, the guitar, the horns, and the cheerful holiday wishes of a blind musician. For years we will believe that every singer wearing sunglasses—Héctor Lavoe, Bobby Womack, Stevie Wonder, Ray Charles, Isaac Hayes—is blind. No one will ever tell us different. We play the record and sing along to a song whose words we do not understand. If he were here, our grandfather could translate. If he were here, our grandfather could love us. Without him we have to make do. We make up the words as we go, singing what we think we hear:

Felice la di da
Police la di da
Fleece na vee dah
Potato I know
Blah blah blah blah

We sing louder and louder until our grandmother yells from the kitchen that we are giving her a headache. And still we don't stop.

We're as happy as a song can make us. We sing with gusto, with all the joy the horns can blare. Our bodies help us keep time. We strum our stomachs in tune with the guitar and scratch our forearms to the rhythm of the güiro. We turn empty paper-towel rolls into horns and blow, tooting along with the song. We clasp hands and swing each other round. We're not afraid of looking foolish. No one's watching us.

We belt out, "I wanna wish you a merry Christmas from the bottom of my heart!" and dance around the living room to wish our furniture well. We sing and circle the living room with our arms flung wide. We fling love from our hearts to the corner of the room where our tree stands, dripping garland and tinsel and shatterproof balls, multicolored electric lights blinking back at us in response. We let everything present—the stereo sound system, the love seat and sofa, the coffee and end tables—know how much we love it. We love the flattened arms of our couches, the dust in the corners, all the loose straw from our broom, even the gouges on the floor made from moving the couch and tables out of the way—yes, we love it all.

We dance ourselves dizzy; we sing until we drop. Only then do we hear someone knocking on our door. Our grandmother hushes us before she lets in Ramona, our next-door neighbor.

"Eggnog!" we cheer when Ramona enters, holding a pitcher of white frothy liquid and a pair of plastic cups. We don't tell her we already have a tall can of nog in the cupboard—hers is fresh and we're not stupid. We paw her and clamor as she holds the pitcher high above our heads, defending it with her good hand. "¡Cálmense, niños! Be good," she says. "This is not eggnog."

"What is it?" we ask.

"Coquito. It's much, much better."

"It looks like eggnog," we say.

"It has no eggs," she explains.

Our grandmother relieves Ramona of her pitcher and takes it to the kitchen table, where she has just laid out our breakfast. "It's like a Puerto Rican eggnog," our grandmother tells us.

That's all we need to hear. We'll drink Puerto Rican eggnog and pretend we're in Puerto Rico, just the way we drink Canada Dry and pretend we're in Canada. We can't wait.

We all take our places at the kitchen table. In unison, the two women drop their heavy bodies onto the plastic-covered chairs. Both dressed in floral housedresses and felt slippers, they look like sisters. One woman Puerto Rican and the other woman previously married to one, they visit each other often, coming together over all they have in common. Brought together by their circumstances, women who moved to these projects after their divorces and found themselves living across the hall from each other, they are the best of friends.

Ramona pours only two cups of the coquito, leaving us out. We look up from our milk and toast and eggs and complain. "What about us?"

"You can't have any," our grandmother says. "It has rum in it."

"The best rum there is." Ramona holds her cup beneath our noses. "Smell that?"

We sniff deeply and pull back, choking, feeling as if our nose hairs have been set on fire. "Puerto Rican rum. It puts hair on your chest." Ramona thumps her chest with the hand that's missing two fingers and tells us about the Bacardí factory back in San Juan. She says they give tours where you see large metal drums of the different rums. She says that just standing inside the factory is enough to make you light-headed and drunk.

Ramona says, "¡Salud!" and the two women clink cups.

Our grandmother drinks deeply of the coquito, leans back in her chair, and sighs. "Now that hits the spot."

Ramona pulls a pack of cigarettes from the pocket of her housedress, shakes out two, and hands one over to our grandmother. The women go to the stove to light their cigarettes. Our grandmother knows she shouldn't be smoking; we know it too. We cock our brows as she bends to the burner and lights her cigarette in the flames. At our look, she shrugs and says, "It's Christmas." She drags on the cigarette and takes her time exhaling. "You've got your present and I've got mine."

At the kitchen table, the two women turn their backs on us to keep the smoke away while we finish breakfast. As they trade talk about their children, all at work today earning time and a half, we nudge our grandmother's cup away from her and edge it over to us. We take turns sipping the sweet, strong, creamy coconut drink while the women aren't looking. That first sip is the sweetest thing we have ever tasted; that second sip is the strongest—it burns the backs of our throats, searing a path straight down to our stomachs. We sip and hum and buzz with coconut and rum. The rum snakes its way through our bodies, filling our heads, numbing our tongues to fuzz, relaxing our limbs. We want to lay our ballooning heads down on the table as our bodies fill with a slow-building warmth.

"If we were in Puerto Rico right now, we would all still be asleep," Ramona says. "The parrandas would have kept us up all night." She tells us of late-night parties, of bands of friends showing up to sing and play music outside people's homes during the holiday. She looks over her shoulder, sees us with the coquito, and winks.

"Like Christmas carols?" we ask. Under her gaze we take her cup and drink that too.

"Not really. We let the people in. They're not strangers. We open our homes, give them food and drink. Then we join them and go to the next house. It's fun. Right now we would just be waking up out of our beds," she says, her words carrying us away to the place where she and our grandfather are from, an island we don't expect to ever see.

"There wouldn't be any room for us there," our grandmother says. "He doesn't live alone." Back in Puerto Rico, our grandfather has another wife and a whole other set of children, a sister and brother our mother doesn't know, an aunt and uncle we've never even met.

Ramona asks, "Do you think he'll call?"

"He'd have to care to do that," our grandmother says, blowing out a wreath of smoke. She turns and catches us with the coquito. She looks into both cups. Yes, it is true. We drank every drop. She warns, "You'll both be sorry later."

We're halfway to sorry now. The rum is doing us in. By the

time our mother gets home we'll be quiet as mice. Tipsy and languid, we'll hunker down in the back bedroom to watch Christmas shows. Curled up on our grandmother's bed, we'll fall asleep to the TV. We'll dream of Rudolph and Frosty, of George Bailey and Bedford Falls. But just now, our lungs expand like bellows, our chests and stomachs grow as warm as radiators, and we feel a surge of energy. Now we have lightning in our veins, thunder in our hearts.

Our grandmother shoos us away. "Get out from underfoot," she tells us. "Go play with your present."

In the living room, we put our record back on. Shy now with our neighbor present, we sit quietly on the couch and merely listen to the music, letting Feliciano sing alone.

"But you hate this song," we hear Ramona say.

"It's just the one day," our grandmother answers. We're neither old nor sensitive enough to guess this song could cause her pain, so we play our record again. And again. And again.

Ramona says, "They're going to wear it out."

Our grandmother jokes, "One can only hope."

The two women laugh until one starts coughing. Ramona comes to us in the living room and says, "Go and get your abuela's inhaler."

We race to the back bedroom, fighting over who will find it the fastest. I win, finding it on the dresser on the other side of the oxygen tank. We run back to the kitchen with the inhaler and watch our grandmother take the puffs that calm her breathing, penance for her cigarette.

"Good job, nena," Ramona tells me, rubbing a circle on my back. She pulls handfuls of sweets from the pockets of her housedress, showering us with packets of dulce de leche, sesame, and tamarind candies. On her way out, she bends to us and kisses our cheeks with lips coco-sweet.

We save our candy for later. Too long have we been away from our record. By now, our mother has caught the A train heading down to Brooklyn and is on her way home to us. We've got a half hour tops before the album goes back into hiding.

Our voices return with our neighbor's departure. We sing once more, this time even louder. We wonder if our grandfather is sitting at home in his living room on an island with his other family, listening to this record today just like we are. We sing to make him miss us, to remember what he's left behind. We sing at the top of our lungs, hoping our voices will carry out to sea, hoping he can hear us across the ocean that keeps us all apart.

Thankful Chinese

We don't do it that way—with spoon rests and place mats and linen napkins, with everyone all together and please pass the salt and all those thank-yous. We're hungry. We don't have time for how was your day and wait till your father gets home and say grace first and did you remember to wash your hands.

The food has been sitting in the bags on the counter for the past ten minutes while she sets the table and makes everything ready, turning jars into cups and paper towels into napkins. When we lift the first bag, the bottom gives way, wet and soggy from all of that special sauce. Tonight there's Chinese, which means shrimp fried rice and chicken and broccoli, egg rolls and soda free with purchase.

We tear right in, dumping out the contents of the cartons onto our paper plates, fighting over who gets the soy sauce and who's stuck with the duck sauce or, worse, the Chinese mustard. We slip the fortunes from their cookies, then toss them without reading; we already know our future. Even *we* don't eat the fortune cookies; we crush them in our fists, pulverizing cookie to powder and licking those crumbles clean.

(When she goes for the TV, we pick out the onions and bean sprouts and slide them back into the carton.)

We rip soy sauce packets open with our teeth, squirting inky sauce all over. It stains the tablecloth, brown dots obliterating the pattern of faded flowers and fruit clusters. We cover the stains with our plates. If we can make it through dinner without her seeing, we'll be all right. Otherwise, it will be some long song about how there is no time to do more laundry; about how much detergent costs; about how messy we two are; about how she is low both on quarters and patience and has no time to put up with this, with us.

We turn on the TV, wheel it to the head of the table, and eat to *The Cosby Show*. We don't look down at our plates; we can't keep our eyes off those Huxtables making their way into the special dining room hidden behind the stairs, the one they hardly ever use, the one they save for special occasions, like when Denise chose a college and Elvin proposed to Sondra. There is Cliff bringing in the turkey on the silver cart with wheels. Everyone—Theo, Vanessa, Sondra, Denise, even Rudy—sits so pretty and fine and thankful and neat and clean, eating at places set with just them in mind, dressed in their best and never spilling.

Before

Watch them, they say—the parents, the aunts and uncles, the grands and guardians. They hand us off to the Olders—our cousins and siblings, play and real—as they pack purses, shine shoes, brush off hats, and put on their Sunday best, although it is only Wednesday. Tonight they have Bible study, usher's meetings, choir practice, Masons and Eastern Stars, things they refuse to miss on our account.

They assign the Olders to keep an eye on us—the big brothers and sisters, the cousins, both play and real. The Olders draw lots and sacrifice two of their own, tribute to the gods that are we. A play cousin to watch us outside, a real cousin to watch us upstairs. At our age we wield power; we exude danger. We are unpredictable. There is no telling what we might do if left to our own devices. We might turn on the stovetop and watch the flames dance up to the ceiling. We might run the water too hot for our baths and scald ourselves to death. We might ignore the Mr. Yuk warnings and rummage through the kitchen cabinets looking for a poisonous drink. We might pick up the receiver, make long-distance calls, and run the bill sky high. We might take candy from a stranger.

They ply us with Mike and Ikes and Lemonheads, Jolly

Ranchers and Boston Baked Beans, Now and Laters and Chick-O-Sticks. They plug in the Ataris, pull out the Teddy Ruxpin and Cabbage Patch dolls, the Voltrons and Transformers, the He-Man and She-Ra action figures, the Jems and G.I. Joes. They hand out jump ropes, marbles, skelly caps, clumps of colored chalk. Anything to distract us from what they are doing. They don't want us to follow when they creep down to the basement and pull out their records, don't want us to see when they usher in friends.

The girlfriend of an older brother—someone who didn't know the music would carry up from the basement and cry out the porch windows on the first landing and flow out onto the sidewalks where we skipped rope, played skelly, and leaped hop-scotch, who had no idea that the music would float up the stairs to the second floor where we huddled on the corner of the bed closest to the TV, joysticks in hand and pressed down on the red firing button to shoot the asteroids and alien centipedes that poured from the top of the screen—puts on the first record and forgets to close the basement door.

The music calls and we come. We bring our young bodies down to the basement door, to the mouth of the forbidden party.

This is no place for little kids, they warn, but we don't budge. Couldn't we cut them a break and just go back upstairs or go outside? Wasn't it enough that they couldn't escape us all day long inside the house, that they were forced to take us with them wherever they went, that we followed and shadowed and mirrored everything they did, that we copied them, and the grown-ups thought it was all so cute? Couldn't they just have a little time alone with kids their own age without us tagging along, dogging their every step?

Ha ha.

"We'll tell." We say the magic words, no qualms about playing dirty.

"You guys are a real pain, you know," they say, in voices filled with all the angst of teenager-ness.

We know. We are the younger ones, born to be the brats. We expect to have everything our way. We have never been disappointed.

They guide us down into the darkened basement, which has been changed over into a teenage nightclub. We forget we are unwanted as soon as we see the spread. The washer's lid is covered in a towel fresh from the line, a makeshift tablecloth to hold the opened packages of Rolos and Krackel bars, our Halloween candy gone missing. Six-packs of root beer and cream soda and bowls of popcorn, pretzels, and potato chips top the dryer. Nothing impressive; nevertheless, we are impressed.

Someone changes the record. The new song tells us to dance, to shout, to shake our bodies down to the ground. We obey. We know a different version of the singer—the Jheri-curled, white-suited, open-shirted, posing-with-a-baby-tiger version. Not the one from before, the one who sang and performed with his brothers. This song is from before everything we know; before the singer's hair caught fire while filming a Pepsi commercial; before the white spangled glove and the military outfits; before he started keeping company with Brooke Shields, a chimpanzee, and that midget kid from *Webster*. This is a before we want to live in, to cling to, to clutch, and to capture. This is before the inevitable end of the evening, when the cars pull up and the lights turn on and we scramble up the stairs as others scramble out the basement door; before the inevitable end of our youth, when the ones watching us grow up grow apart from us; before they move away and leave us behind, returning only for holidays;

before the house grows empty and cold without them—the cousins and siblings, play and real, who watched us when we weren't looking; before the parents, aunts and uncles, grands and guardians string latchkeys onto lanyards and drape them around our necks, the way Leia did to Luke and Han in the ceremony at the end of *Star Wars* that somehow made destroying the Death Star akin to winning the Olympics. Before they say to us, "You're old enough now to stay at home on your own," and pretend we've won a prize, caparisoning us in adolescence. Before we bow our heads like Han and Luke, waiting to receive the latchkey, knowing that, in fact, we've won nothing.

Surely Not

Surely not *everybody* was kung fu fighting, but we were. Rained in on a Saturday afternoon in late summer, we have nowhere to go. It's a cleaning day—our beds are stripped. Our mother sweeps us from our rooms, down the hall, and into the living room, where she cordons us off and mops us in.

We settle on the couch in front of the floor-model TV just in time for Kung Fu Theater. Today's feature is *Mortal Combat* a.k.a. *The Return of the 5 Deadly Venoms* a.k.a. *Crippled Avengers*. Rapt, we watch the Tian Nan Tigers kill Tu Tin To's wife and chop off his young son's arms. Riveted, we watch him avenge his family by crippling everyone he meets, blinding a peddler, rendering a blacksmith deaf and mute, and cutting off the legs of an innocent bystander.

Our mother returns to check on us, sees the screen, and warns us not to fight.

She says, "Remember your age."

Says, "Remember your strength."

She says, "She's not as old as you, or as big."

Says, "No roughhousing."

But what else is there for us to do?

We play all the parts. We wander the living room pretending to be deaf, dumb, and blind. Holding broomsticks out before us, we feel our way, toppling furniture as we go. We want to be crippled. We want a teacher to take us in, train us, and make us strong. We want iron fists, iron legs. We want to be avenged.

We size each other up, circling for our attacks, looking for openings. We limit ourselves to Tiger style only. We chop and kick and push and claw. We evade and sidestep and duck and block.

We knock something over and our mother runs in and scruffs us, grabbing us by the necks like we're kittens, shaking us until we rattle.

"She's not a boy," she says. "I told you not to play so rough!"

We blink, uncomprehending.

"Do you hear me? She's not your brother!"

We hear her loud and clear, but the words, they make no sense. What is a boy, what is a girl?—we are simply siblings. I'm his brother; he is my sister. He is my brother; I'm his sister. When I bite into his arm hard enough to break the skin, the blood that surfaces is my own; I taste my blood metal and we are the same.

She looks me over as she scolds, turning my face this way and that. "You don't know your own strength," she tells him. But *I* do and it is no bother. Brotherlove only makes a girl stronger.

We're back at it again as soon as she leaves. "I'll go easier on you," he says.

"I won't," I promise.

Heedless of our mother's warning, we fight. We fight because it's Saturday afternoon and our Tiger style is weak, and we have to make it better. We fight because this is how we love, and our time together is running out. At summer's end, he's heading off to a boarding school in New England. He'll take the Amtrak at

Penn Station and go to a place where I can't follow. What's worse than any pain is being without him, and what's worse even still is that it's his idea to go. He's studied for this place, taken tests to get in. I am never scared that he'll hurt me, but his leaving is another thing.

With my head locked under his arm he tells me, "I'm really going to miss this," but I know that's not true, and knowing how ready, how eager, he is to leave me behind lends fury to my fists, making it easy to break his hold and topple him down onto the couch, to throw myself across him and brace my forearm against his throat. "You'll go and forget me there," I say. "You won't ever come back."

Pinned beneath me, he stares up at me and says, "You never have to be scared of that." He says, "You worry over nothing," but in fact, it is a little bit frightening.

You'll Go

ecause it's for your own good. Because it's a way out. Because your parents say so—they want the best for you and you have no say in the matter. Because reading is fundamental and a mind is a terrible thing to waste. Because other families would kill for their kids to attend private school for free, because only fools leave money on the table and your mama didn't raise no fool. Because they gave the aptitude tests to everyone in your fifth-grade gifted class and you were the only one—the only one!—to pass the months-long battery of tests and you can't let everyone down now. Because the entire school is counting on you—the principal made a special announcement over the loudspeaker on the last day of class just to offer you congratulations. Because your teachers are oh-so-proud.

You say, "But it won't be any fun without my friends."

"Mark my words," your mother says, "in a few years, these same kids you love so much will be out here doing the same old same old, and you'll have gone places."

The place you are meant to go is a fancy private school on the Upper East Side whose tuition costs more than your parents make in a year. Your brain will get you in and pay the way. All you have to do is attend an intensive summer enrichment program open to genius, underprivileged, minority kids from all five boroughs. If you can complete the program without getting cut, a scholarship awaits. There will be uniforms, book allowances, and tuition fee waivers in your future—the whole full ride.

You'll go all summer long. Five mornings a week a bus will pick you up before the neighborhood awakens and bring you back each night, and in the hours in between you will be enriched. Your parents call it the chance of a lifetime, but they're too old to remember how a whole lifetime can be lived in one short sweet summer.

They say, "You don't know just how good you have it."

So what if the program costs you your summer? So what if being enriched means that you rise earlier than your parents, leaving each day in darkness and returning home to the same, and you never feel the sun warm on your shoulders or the backs of your knees, and you forget the heat of the concrete sidewalk burning through the bottoms of your plastic jellies when you run too fast in a game of tag? So what if there is no tag and there is no hanging out on stoops, no splashing at the public pool, and no hogging the swings at the park, and in your absence your friends forget you?

"Stop studying these kids," your father warns. "They're not going anywhere."

But you know exactly where they're going. Each day they're going to the public school for free lunch and then they're heading out to play. They're scouring the streets for phone repairmen so they can cop telephone wire for double Dutch. They're squirting water guns, lighting firecrackers at the curbs, and chalking the streets for games of skelly. They're buying ten-cent flavored ice pops from the corner bodega, pushing the frozen liquid out from its long clear sleeve and into their mouths, staining their tongues all the colors of the rainbow. They're playing follow-the-leader and crack-the-whip. And they're doing it all without you.

"Trust us," your parents say. They predict that one day you'll thank them. They say that one day you will understand.

If only you'd known last summer that there would never be another one of its kind, that come this summer you'd be too busy with books and school to run with your friends through the fire hydrant and feel the cold gush of water on your hot bare legs. You'd have cheered louder when someone's uncle came out brandishing a wrench to open the fire hydrant. You'd have laughed longer when your friends splashed the approaching cars and drenched each other when those cars were out of sight. When it was your turn to be soaked you'd have let the water hit you full blast instead of putting up your hands and running to the stoop for cover. Because now, when the bus drops you off at night and you slump toward home, the sun is down and the hydrant is closed and the gutters and curbs are dry and there's no water anywhere, not even the hint of a trickle.

We Wonder
(Ode to Lisa Lisa)

... If we take you home, if our parents will kill us, or if they'll ever know; if our latchkeys are just the thing to help make this a go; if we should wait till they're asleep, or just do it when they're not at home, which is always. If they catch us it's all over. As soon as they get home from work they put us under lock and key. They don't want us to suffer what's happened to them—young lives over before they even have a chance to begin.

... Will you still be in love, baby? Or if you even are. You don't exactly say so when you call us over from your car and drive slowly to keep by our side, offering us rides, as we run the errands on which we've been sent. What we hear is "Yo, shorty!" "Excuse me, miss," and jokes about jam versus jelly, all clues that one summer has made all the difference. We've traded in our short sets for tank tops and Daisy Dukes, and we're women now—or at least on the brink, but we don't think anyone notices but you. At home we make ourselves useful. We pick up the dry cleaning. We babysit our younger siblings and make them after-school snacks. We kill the mice. We take out the trash. We want so badly to matter, and whenever we come outside, your whistles and cat-calls make us feel seen, so, so flattered. Hanging out on the stoop with your boys, or leaning against your car, or just loitering by the pay phones, your eyes are on us, dogging our steps, watching us everywhere we go until it's so we can't escape the reach of those long gazes in a neighborhood that's only so big. All of this attention goes to our heads.

Because we need you tonight, we'll wait till it's way past dark to sneak out to the park and cut across the bleachers. We'll do our best to blend in among everyone who's old enough to be here, until you finally call us over. We let you lead us to your Mazda, your Jeep, your Escalade, your Range Rover. We let you adjust the passenger seat and tilt us all the way back till we're lying flat just like we're at home in our own beds. We take your advice and close our eyes—we don't worry our pretty little heads. "Just relax, baby girl," is what you say when your hand grips our thigh and you pretend to play with the fringe on our cutoffs. But the hand on our thigh climbs higher and higher—so high!—as your fingers dig and poke and pry. We fight the urge—we don't cry. You say *relax* as we squirm. You say *relax* though you can see it hurts. We wonder if it's too late for us to say *stop*, too late to say *please don't*. Will you still be in love, baby? No, of course you won't.

Summer Says

ummer says, "Release them," and our teachers let us go, relinquishing us to the summer and the vacation that with it comes.

The last bell of the school year rings and the big green metal doors spring open and unleash us out onto the world. Goodbye to our public elementary school, that brown brick building with its windows all welded shut. No more crossing guards, morning lineups, fire drills, after-school programs, bullhorns, and loudspeakers. No more bells to guide our days. Now we follow only the sun.

Like expeditioners we leave at first light, sure to take only the most necessary of supplies. Jacks, chalk, jump ropes, and fireworks—all the things we carry are all the things we need to see us through the day. There'll be no going back and forth, no running in and out. If we show our faces before the sun goes down, we'll be deemed underfoot and forced to stay inside, condemned to an afternoon of *General Hospital* and Luke and Laura, *All My Children* and Erica Kane, Tattoo ringing the bell in the tower on *Fantasy Island* and crying, "The plane, the plane!"—trapped indoors and sentenced to watching soap operas and sitcoms with grown-ups while just outside our freedom, our friends, and our summer await.

All summer we have the days to ourselves, the neighborhood to ourselves, and the streets are ours for the taking. Each morning we are few, but by afternoon we are legion. With each block our numbers grow as we ring buzzers to free our friends and shout up to windows for parents to send them down. By midday, the pockets of our short sets drag, heavy with the quarters and half-dollars earned running errands for old folks, carrying bags up the stoops or racing back and forth to the corner store and being told to keep the change. We spend that change on plunder, splurging on all the bags of cheese curls and packs of Now and Laters our stomachs can hold. We devour boxes of Lemonheads and Mike and Ikes, turning the empty boxes into kazoos and trumpeting them down the street until we find an open hydrant and drink our fill.

Each summer we are fewer than we were the year before. Summer deals us all different hands; flying some of our friends out of LaGuardia and JFK and shuttling them off to Barbados, Jamaica, Puerto Rico, and Trinidad, sending them to islands where their parents or grandparents were born and where relatives they barely know stand ready to take them in; whisking others away through the Fresh Air Fund, sending them off to the country to breathe the unpolluted air, ride horses, and live with rich rural white families; and keeping others busy with new adultlike chores. The chore-doers brush past us, pushing shopping carts filled with laundry bundled into black garbage bags or lugging bags of groceries on their way back from Key Food, eyes blank of recognition, faces gaunt with early adulthood, necks encircled by lanyards from which dangle gleaming latchkeys.

We are what is left when the dust of everyone else's leaving clears.

You could say that we're the lucky ones, free to roam, to soak up the summer and bask in its burn. No one sends for us and we have nothing to do except for everything we want, and all we want is to leave our mark and remind the neighborhood that we are here. From Linden Boulevard to East Ninety-Eighth Street and East New York Avenue to Van Sinderen where the L train crosses with the 3 on its way to Canarsie, this world is ours. The only thing special about it is that it belongs to us and we belong to it. No one loves it like we do. Not the adults who pass it by as they fold themselves into cars or disappear up the steps to the elevated train each morning. They hurry past the neighborhood, but we peer into its every corner and baptize each and every block. Every curb demands our attention, every broken slab of sidewalk and every patch of dirt that births the weeds that break through deserves our notice. We tramp through every abandoned lot we find, sidestepping the small colorful vials that appear more and more frequently and become harder and harder to avoid. We cross in between and not at the green. We pat every hydrant on the head. We split every pole. We step on every crack, breaking the backs of mothers everywhere we go. We are vigilant; we keep watch. When an old man totters down the stoop on his way to the check-cashing place on Rockaway and Livonia, we flank him, forming an honor guard to keep away the teenage boys who post up on the corners, who lie in wait by the pay phones, who think that beepers make them men, and who would rob an old man for his SSI and disability checks in a heartbeat. We are a neighborhood army, and we see the old man safely there and we bring him safely home.

We are our own protection and we protect our own.

We tap into the rhythm of our neighborhood and follow where the streets lead us. We take Hopkinson Avenue, pass the public pool, and cross over to the park. Teenagers crowd the benches, flirting and preening and laughing as they raise the volume on the boom boxes at their feet, blaring the soundtrack of summer. This park is no place for sissies. The seesaws, slides, and swings are all metal—everything here burns. Bypassing the baby swings, the jungle gym, and the basketball courts, we claim the grown-up swings for our own, chasing away the younger kids who can't pump themselves but hang around begging for a push. We pair off two to a swing—one to sit and ride, the other to stand and pump. The teenagers and their boom boxes fill the air with song and the music says don't worry be happy, tells us it's our prerogative, reminds us that joy and pain is like sunshine and rain. The swing scorches us with summer as we sit and its metal bottom sears the backs of our legs, as we stand and its metal chains blaze imprints on our palms, but we ride the air and chase the music-filled breeze and the songs soothe all our burns.

We could live on this swing, in this moment, in this summer, but it comes to an end—too soon, too soon. Long before we're ready, the streetlights flicker on, beacons to call us home. Block after block, the lights come on in tandem to guide us back, a trail better than bread crumbs but not at all needed.

We have always known the way home.

The Best That You Can Do

Preferences

Jamie wakes in a bed that is not her own. It is Mikhail's bed and Mikhail's cramped apartment, and tonight is the first night she has ever heard of this name attached to someone young, attractive, and American rather than old, political, and Russian. Mikhail is a grad student at her university, but he is not her TA and they are not on campus, so it is all right.

He has taken her to his place in one of the nearby towns whose name she always forgets. It is either Mountain View or Menlo Park, depending on which way they headed on El Camino.

Drinks in his apartment, seated on his floor near his couch, her back against his chest, his legs on either side of hers, comfortable. Mikhail says he went to the party "on a lark," and she finds the phrase expressive, charming. Jamie is a smart girl, capable of appreciating irony.

Mikhail has no television. Planks of wood balanced on cinder blocks serve as bookshelves. There are more books than shelves to hold them. Books are stacked haphazardly atop each other, splayed open. More than a few are upside down. His many books are haggard with wear and tear. Even from her seat on the floor, she can see the violence that's been done to them. She thought a grad student would have been gentler.

He offers her a back rub.

How easy and innocent it all begins. Thumbs kneading shoulders, pads of flesh digging into skin. A simple whispered question, "Wanna come with me to the back room?"

The moment is so like the one earlier in the evening when— her back braced against the wall and his hands nestled in the back pockets of her jeans—Mikhail nuzzled her and said, "Do you want to go somewhere and maybe have a drink or two?"

She appreciates the way he says *back room* instead of *bedroom*, as if he is inviting her to view a painting and not asking to get lucky. She has already gone this far, but there is a certain point beyond which she will not go. By *this far* she means coming to his place. She has no intention of sleeping with him, however, and to enter his bedroom would make him think otherwise. As though the events of the early evening were not meant to lead up to this, she turns to face him and says, "I would prefer not to."

It sounds more prim than she would like, a guest declining the last deviled egg on a bed of lettuce.

He stops rubbing.

"This is too much like high school," Mikhail says without rancor, meaning *she* is too much like high school. Implying he's been mistaken about her. She isn't, after all, astute enough, modern enough, progressive enough, mature enough.

She is silent. Stiffly, she scoots away from him until her back touches the wall.

On hands and knees he crawls across the carpet to her. "Look," he says. "I'm sorry. I didn't mean it like that."

"It's okay," she mumbles, unwilling to let him know he's hurt her. She smiles weakly to let him see she is not accusing. She is unsurprised when he kisses her; she thinks it's his way of apologizing.

Her clothing does not come off, but articles of clothing are unbuttoned, unzipped, and unfastened. She is askew beneath him on the carpet, covered by his body, pinned by his weight and entangled by his limbs. There is no more kissing, no more rubbing. She is splayed like one of the books on his shelves, handled none too gently. She thinks he mistakes her shaking her head, her resistance, her pushing against him for something else, though what the something else could be she doesn't know.

Afterward.

"May I use your bathroom?"

Without opening his eyes, Mikhail points down the hall.

In Mikhail's bathroom, there is only one washcloth and one bath towel on the rack. No hand towels for guests. Jamie rinses his bar of soap under hot water, then washes her face with her hands. She dries her hands on his towel, seeing the black smudge on her hand, a leftover from the party. They'd marked an X on her hand in Magic Marker so she could reenter the student center at will. At orientation, they warn you about what can happen at a party, what can happen on a date. But she was no longer at the party, and she and Mikhail weren't actually on a date. Technically, tonight counts as nothing. Tonight does not exist.

She feels too tired to go back out to Mikhail's living room. Too tired to see him. Too tired to think. She goes farther down the hallway to his bedroom, where she had not wanted to go before, and curls up on top of his covers. It no longer matters if she is back here.

Sometime later he wakes her and says, "Think I should take you home now."

Jamie rises silently, wordlessly reaching for the thin jacket he's holding for her. Without his help, she slips herself into it and follows him out.

Mikhail opens the car door for her. He asks if she is hungry, if she wants to grab a bite to eat at either Denny's or Jack in the Box, the only two near things open this time of night.

"No. I'm not hungry."

"Sure?" he asks, belatedly solicitous. "It's no trouble. They're both on the way."

"I would prefer not to," she says, wanting only to go "home"— which is how she thinks of her dorm on campus—to her own bed, her own washcloth, and her own bath towel, folding her hands in her lap and looking ahead on El Camino at the oncoming cars with their bright lights winking as if they know her.

Kitler

On Valentine's Day, her boyfriend of six weeks gifted her with a cat. The cat was mostly white, except for the black upper portion of its face and a square black splotch above its lip that made it look like Adolf Hitler. Though her boyfriend pretended not to see the uncanny resemblance, there was no denying it. She thanked him, although she didn't know what to do with the cat, how to care for it—she'd never owned a pet before, not even a goldfish. As soon as he left, she typed *cat* and *Hitler* into a Google search; up sprang a plethora of images—a website even—devoted to cats that looked like Hitler. Kitlers, they were called. She was now the reluctant owner of a Kitler.

She watched the Kitler closely, but it mostly slept, waking only when she played the Police's "Message in a Bottle" while making her daily morning coffee. When Sting got to the part about sending out an SOS, it lifted its furry head, twitched its ears, and stared plaintively, ready to help.

Two weeks after giving her the Kitler, her boyfriend came over unannounced. He accused her of seeing other men, using her absences at their morning workouts as proof. Waking up early to hit the gym had never really been her thing; she'd been there only because of a New Year's resolution. Since receiving the cat, she awakened each day to find it curled atop the blankets, warming her feet. She couldn't rise without dislodging it, and the Kitler liked to sleep late, which—to her—seemed as good a reason as any to skip the gym.

Her boyfriend didn't believe her. There was someone else; he just knew it. He raised his voice. He shook her, and the Kitler wound itself around her feet and vocalized, emitting a keening sound that was a cross between a yowl and a mewl, a yewl. (She'd heard that cats were aloof, but her Kitler was surprisingly compassionate, protective.) He told her to shut the cat up, but the cat was a free spirit—there was no stopping the noise. She told him it was over and asked him to leave; she didn't like to be accused and she didn't like to be shaken. He apologized. He wasn't this kind of guy at all. Loving her made him crazy. It would never happen again. If only she would reconsider.

She would not.

"Just one thing," he said before leaving. "What did you name this cat? You never even told me. You owe me at least that. I bought it for you."

"I haven't named it yet," she said. "I'm not sure I will."

She couldn't have explained it to him, but naming the cat hadn't seemed necessary. Whenever she needed it, it was there. It defended her, protected her, and kept her feet toasty warm at night. She and the Kitler had something deeper, better than names. Between them they needed no names; they understood each other perfectly.

My Mother Wins an Oxygen Tank at the Casino, or, My Mother Makes an Exception

My mother wins an oxygen tank at the casino where she spends all day playing the slots. She's always coming back with free gifts: a revolving spice rack, a cozy all-season comforter, a fondue kit, a set of stemless wineglasses. Things that would make great wedding presents if we knew anybody getting married.

We put the free gifts upstairs in the third bedroom, which used to be my office. The boxes line up on the cheap futon. I stack more gifts on top of the desk and in its matching chair. Soon the boxes cover the floor and I have to tiptoe around them, stepping gingerly like a cat burglar in a movie facing off against laser grids.

"They don't give out things like that," I say.

"Okay, you win." She raises her hands, all *don't shoot*. "I bought it myself. I've always wanted one."

The little green tank gives her nothing but trouble. She doesn't like the way the tubing in her nose traps her, limiting how far she can go, or the way she trips daily over the long cord, or how it kinks and coils into knots she has to take the time to undo.

We sit together in the living room after dinner watching TV and I tease her, saying she looks like Bane from *The Dark Knight Rises*, the third film in Christopher Nolan's Batman reboot.

It's all true.

Except that the doctors put her on oxygen the last time she was in the hospital and said that from now on she has to have it round the clock.

Except that she hasn't been to the casino in years, not since our next-door neighbor who used to drive her there and back died in a nursing home three months after her crazy son committed her just so he could have her house.

Except that she looks nothing like the villain who captured Gotham and held that city by its throat. Sitting on the couch beside me, my mother looks exactly like what she is, a woman slowly being taken away from me, one difficult breath at a time.

Everything

The last time he came by for his stuff hadn't been goodbye at all. She'd gone into her bedroom to retrieve his slippers and he'd followed her in and they'd made love on top of the comforter and he'd left empty-handed. This time he stayed put in her living room, poised on the edge of her armchair.

He'd come back for everything. He wanted it all back, every last thing he'd left behind in her apartment. Closure, he called it. She was a loose thread to be bitten off clean between the teeth. Once he had everything, there'd be no reason to call or come by, no excuse to repeat the last visit's mistake.

Their breakup, he said, was on her. He'd never known a woman to be so selfish.

She returned to the living room with a small box from Amazon. Repurposed from her last book order, it was the smallest box she could find, just the right size to hold all his belongings. "This should do it," she said.

He sprang up from her chair, took the box right out of her hands. But there were just a few things in there, really. Those leather slippers she'd bought for him after he'd stayed over and complained about her cold, uncarpeted floors. The two boxes of peppermint tea she'd purchased because he loved the fresh taste and tingle of mint, though its smell made her ill. One night, after a dinner date, she'd surprised him with a cup of that tea, but he'd complained she'd bought the wrong brand. Just a few things to be returned. The package of individual floss picks she'd bought for him after the first night he slept over—the next morning he'd groused at the way her dental floss tangled when he pulled it from the spool. That blue frosted pint glass from the sports bar arcade they'd ventured into that time he'd picked her up after a delayed flight—the closest place they could find near the airport. There they had eaten fried things and watched college football. Afterward, in the games section, they'd played Skee-Ball, and she'd earned just enough tickets to win him the glass.

"Is that everything?" he asked her, checking to be sure.

Surely he could see that everything fit into the small box. For proof, she withdrew each packed item and, one by one, she replaced them all back snug. The box he held was full. There wasn't room for anything more. There wasn't even room for all there was.

So Good to See You

He spots her at the restaurant in the South Loop Hotel where his company is sponsoring a happy hour. They easily recognize in their adult faces the teenagers they remember.

As luck would have it, they are both single—she recently so, he long since. They agree to meet for lunch the next day. Neither is willing to call it a date, though they both know it has the potential.

They meet the next day on the north side, at the Ann Sather's on Broadway and Granville, an innocuous place she picks for the large cinnamon rolls that come with every order. Two tables are being cleared when they enter; they don't wait long.

After the server pours their coffees and takes their orders, they settle in to the business of catching up.

"Graduation?"

"Fifteen years?" she asks, straining to hear him above the general din. "Was that really the last time we saw each other?"

"I'm not even sure I *did* see you at graduation," he says.

She raises her voice to be heard above the scraping of chairs as the empty table beside them fills with a party of four. "I was on the stage, giving the valedictory speech. You could hardly have missed me."

"Such a go-getter," he says. "Just as I remember."

She takes that as a compliment. "Nothing's changed."

"Nothing ever does." He fiddles with the sugar packets and opens two into his coffee.

"You've lost your hair," she says before tact silences her. "*That's* a change," she laughs, hoping to pass off her comment as a joke. She remembers that he'd wanted to grow his hair into dreadlocks back when it was the style, but his mother had made him keep it cut low and close to his scalp to prevent him from looking like riffraff. He'd been standing last night, but now that they are both seated, and he's leaning across the table, the horseshoe outline on his scalp is unmistakable, making him look years older than his age.

She looks at the time on her cell phone and pretends to remember another engagement. She is running late, she says. She's only got a half hour, tops.

He ignores the way her eyes skip over his face, no longer appraising. He won't let her off that easy. He'd put on cologne for this lunch. "You look beautiful as ever, so *that* hasn't changed," he says, knowing a compliment will buy him extra time.

But it's true; she *is* as beautiful as she ever was. Her face is less youthful, but it is the face her other face had been leaning toward. Fifteen years ago, as a senior in high school, her features had hinted at what her face would become, but he had not been around since to see the changes. He was jealous now of the years he'd been robbed of looking at her, jealous of those who'd had the pleasure. Had these others known this was the face she would finally wear? Had they seen her too large, too wide smile and known it would one day fit her face, that her chin would lengthen and become firmer, a shelf for the smile she hid from the catcallers and saved only for those she knew, the smile that had offered him a friendship he'd been too prideful to accept? Had he settled for her friendship long ago, maybe it could have blossomed into more and he could have had all those years to watch her face grow into the one before him.

The server brings their orders, a garden omelet for her and an open-faced hot turkey sandwich for him with mashed potatoes and gravy.

What are they doing with their lives now?

"I guess you could call me a drug dealer," he tells her. She cuts into her omelet and waits for the punch line.

He tells her he's a project manager for a pharmaceutical company and she laughs at his joke. Her laughter, a sharp sweet stab, slices through him like the wind off Lake Michigan that comes in through his car windows when he is on Lake Shore Drive, whipping tears from his eyes, stinging him awake.

She's an obstetrician, the doctor she's always wanted to be. She's in town for a few days to confer with a colleague at Northwestern with whom she is working on a book about women's health. Together they eat and remember the things they've escaped. The South Side was supposed to claim their lives. He was supposed to become a drug dealer and she was supposed to wind up pregnant.

He lifts his coffee cup. "A toast to not being what they predicted."

"To beating the odds."

They laugh and clink cups. "I guess we showed them," he says. He asks what she's been up to and she mentions recent trips to sub-Saharan Africa, to Cameroon and Somaliland to help prevent infant mortality. She talks of combining work with volunteerism, of training midwives and birthing attendants. She rhapsodizes about birthing kits, small biodegradable baggies filled with the essentials—disposable razor, twine, alcohol swab, gloves, gauze—to ensure sanitary deliveries in the bush. He drinks his coffee and slices his turkey, running it through the gravy and mashed potatoes before forking it into his mouth. He chews and listens intently, unsure how to respond. He wonders if she wants a donation.

"Enough about me. How have *you* been?"

"Can't complain," he says, wincing at his paltry answer. He wishes he had more to say—wishes that he were the owner of the pharmaceutical company rather than one of its many managers, or that he too had ended up being the doctor he said he would.

A dribble of gravy smears his tie, and he dips his napkin into his water glass and dabs at the stain, trying to catch it before it sets. By the time he has sponged off the gravy, his remorse has dissipated, replaced with confusion over the coolness of his reception. She's in town until Monday, but she hasn't told him which hotel she's staying in, asked him for his phone number, or invited him over. He's accustomed to women who make themselves readily available, who make it easy. And why shouldn't they? He could be in jail; he could be a deadbeat dad; he could be dead. He is none of these things. He's a good catch. He has a degree, a job, a condo, and a car. Maybe he's no Barack Obama, but he's doing well enough that he need not make excuses for himself. If she doesn't think he is enough, there are plenty of other women out there. He can have his pick.

He says, "Life has been good to me," and settles back in his chair. He fans his tie to make the wet spot dry faster. "I've got a real good life."

"So I see," she says, agreeing merely to be agreeable.

The good life is evident in his slight paunch, his full face, a portrait of mediocrity. The aroma of his self-satisfaction wafts off him like the scent of someone fresh from the gym. She remembers him claiming that black men were an endangered species, bragging that he was defying the odds simply by being alive, and arguing that anything else he did counted as extra. That had been his excuse not to take the AP courses in biology and chemistry with her and his reasoning not to apply himself to his studies. He was too easily contented; it was why she had wanted only friendship. She doesn't deny that there's a war on black men, but she knows men who have done far more than he has with far, far less.

She finishes her omelet and signals the server for the check.

He tells her of trips to Vegas, Brazil, and the Dominican Republic. He's going to Jamaica next year. He hears it's nice over there, a virtual paradise.

"That's true," she says. "I was there last summer training doctors and NICU specialists."

"All work and no play, or did you get to have any fun?"

"Some." She bites into her cinnamon roll, licks the icing from her fingers, and asks what he does in his spare time.

He has tickets to all the games. Blackhawks, Bulls, Cubs. "The Cubbies are going to win it this year," he predicts.

She remembers him riding north to the Addison stop with his father to catch the Cubs games at Wrigley Field. She is still a Sox fan, but she'll take a Chicago win any way she can get it. A World Series win and the election of the country's first woman president would make it a banner year indeed. "Do you tell yourself that every year?" she asks.

"This time it's true."

The server brings their check on a small, lacquered tray and places it in front of him. When he doesn't reach for it, she lays down enough cash to cover her half of the bill plus tip. He scoops up the cash and leaves his credit card.

"It was great, really great, but I've got to head up to Evanston," she says, rising to leave. This time he doesn't try to stop her. She's going to catch the red line down the block and take it to Howard, where she can switch over to the purple line to get to Northwestern. She still knows the way.

His car is parked outside at a meter, but he doesn't offer her a ride. "It was good to see you," he says.

"So good," she agrees.

Neither mentions keeping in touch.

She leaves him at the table, waiting for the server to return his card. She is glad she's had the chance to see him. Though she hadn't wanted to risk their friendship on a romance, she'd always wondered what could have been between them, what had become of him, what he had ultimately become.

She is glad to finally know.

Forgive Me

I lost my mother's red plastic heart sunglasses when I was seven. She used to wear them with a pair of dark denim pedal pushers whose seams were stitched with bloodred thread. Above she wore a red-and-white-striped shirt with a pleated front and little flutter cap sleeves. Below she wore strappy red leather sandals. In the middle, a red webbed belt—the kind worn by Boy Scouts and soldiers. It was 1982. She was the most beautiful thing.

I lived with her only on the weekends. During the week, my grandmother's old sour sister kept me and took me to school, but on the weekends my mother made up for our time apart. She made me pancakes for breakfast and let me try on her clothes, pulling one Pierre Cardin shirt after another over my small head. She let me whirl her tams like I was making pizza dough. She let me borrow her sunglasses and wear them to school.

What can I say? All second graders like bright new things, and every girl in class wanted to try on my mother's shades. We passed them up and down our rows of desks until the teacher snatched them away.

My mother forgave me as soon as I called and told her what happened, but I kept crying into the receiver until my old sour aunt took the phone from me. It's almost forty years since those sunglasses went missing, yet the guilt still lingers, plaguing me over breakfast. I pour our bowls of cereal and apologize once again when my mother passes me the carton of milk. Yes, we live together now.

If only I hadn't lost them, we might not be where we are today. My mother thinks I mean the current presidency. She thinks I mean the masks, the virus, the quarantine, and all the police brutality. Which, of course, I do. But also, the way I'm afraid to lose anything to this very day, which also means that I'm afraid to hold on tight, which also means that I'm afraid to have, which also means that I'd just rather not.

My mother asks, "Why do you think you're responsible for all the woes of the world? Why do you think everything is your fault?"

"Isn't it?"

Dutch

She's only five minutes away from her apartment when the fuel light comes on, but she pulls into the service station anyway, too cautious to risk it. Motorcycles are parked in a row by the defunct public pay phone, their riders loitering on the curb around the corner and out of the attendant's sight. Cases of window solvent, bundles of firewood, and canisters of propane are lined up in front of the station. The station's windows advertise the price of milk, offer deals on coffee. Cigarettes are $11.29. She remembers when they were as low as $2.89, though she can no longer recall the taste of nicotine. She parks at the pump and heads inside to pay. She prefers the personal touch. She still makes phone calls, writes letters, sends cards—she never texts. *Old lady*, her friends tease her. *Relic*, they call her to her face.

The door is locked this late at night. Barricaded behind a bulletproof window, crowded in by packs of cigarettes, gum, and condoms, waits an attendant whose name is full of more consonants than she can decipher. She greets him, but he's deaf until she asks for twenty on pump five. He pushes out a clear plastic drawer. She reaches into her handbag for her cash, and out with it comes an old receipt. She drops a twenty into the drawer. The attendant retracts it, rings her up, and turns away.

After filling up, she replaces the cap and nozzle. Back in her car, she holds the receipt to the overhead light. It's from last October, from her last date with her last boyfriend. Ink smudged from too much handling, the restaurant's receipt is all a blur, the tally and tip too faint to read.

What an awful night that night had been. Who would guess that offering to pay for herself would have wreaked such havoc? She'd been trying to present herself as a partner, but he'd accused her of emasculation. Insulted, he'd left her there at the restaurant, alone at the table with the check she'd tried to split.

She balls the receipt, stuffing it into her cup holder before pulling out of the station. She can't remember how much her half had been, and the blurred total won't say, but she doesn't need it to know what that meal cost her. She is paying still.

Why Not?

Why shouldn't she agree to dinner? She's known him ever since she moved to Philadelphia for grad school. For years she saw him at the various service projects for which she volunteered. Year after year she stood beside him at the Salvation Army on Girard Avenue on Thanksgiving Day, scooping spoonfuls of stuffing, greens, and candied yams onto paper plates to serve hot meals to the homeless. For years she ran into him at the Odunde Festival and at the Urban League, encountering him at all the places young black professionals frequented for fun, networking, and fellowship. They are nonspeaking acquaintances—they have friends in common but have never been introduced or ever had a conversation.

So why not? Grad school has come and gone and has been followed by a job in Chicago, but she's back in Philly now to promote her latest book. She's in town for a week of public readings, book signings, and radio shows. She's posted flyers on social media and sent out Facebook invites, and many of her old friends have come out to support.

He appears at her Sunday afternoon event in North Philly, where seventy guests cram into a venue meant to hold only fifty. After she's finished her reading and the applause has ended and she's signed everyone's copies, a few friends linger and make plans with her. He lingers too, speaking to the friends he also knows. As the venue's staff begin to fold and stack the chairs, he holds out his book to her. "Just one more?"

"Of course." She props his book against the podium and signs the title page in a bold scrawl.

"Are you booked all week for lunch?" he asks, gesturing at her departing friends.

"Looks that way," she says.

"Then how about dinner?"

Why not? It's just one simple meal. After all, she's having lunch with everyone else. She agrees and gives him her phone number, thinking nothing of it until he shows up with a freshly washed car, a haircut, a suit, and a polish on his shoes.

When he opens her passenger door, she asks, "Is this a date?"

"I wasn't sure," he says, closing the car door behind her. "But I was hoping."

It's Restaurant Week and he's chosen a nice one in Ritten-house Square with a pianist who plays the soul ballads of the seventies. How can she know that this pleasant evening will not be worth the heartache (on his end) and the tedium (on hers) that follows close behind? Right now she's giddy after a success-ful event, warmed by friendships still intact, soothed by soft ro-mantic lighting, and flattered by male attention. He confesses that he's noticed her for years and has always wanted to get to know her better, tells her that he saw her flyer on Facebook after it had been shared by a friend of a friend and that even though that friend had canceled at the last minute he'd decided to come anyway and he's so glad he did. How can she guess that once she flies back to Chicago this man, sitting across from her so innocently buttering a roll, will inundate her with phone calls riddled with dull conversation? When he calls, he doesn't ask a single thing about her, doesn't try to get to know her. Calling every night without actually having anything to say, he talks to her as if they are an old married couple rather than two people who have been on only one date. He calls to tell her what he's making for dinner. He calls to tell her that he's fixing his fence. He calls, each time expecting her to drop whatever she's doing and give him her undivided attention because he paid for their date and now believes she owes him all of her time. When she asks if there's anything about her he would like to know, he asks, "Do you wear high heels to work?" When she asks him about his interests, his background, his family, he tells her he's an army brat, but instead of describing the places he's lived or offering something meaningful about an itinerant adolescence, he talks about badge bunnies. Disclosing how women with a thing for men in uniform hang around military bases hoping to entrap officers, he regales her with stories of his soldier father's extramarital affairs. After two weeks of nightly calls like this, he invites her back east to attend his aunt and uncle's silver anniversary party, saying, "I want to show off our relationship." That they are in a relationship is news to her.

Who can guess that her hesitation, her confusion, will cause the same friends who dolled up for her book signing to castigate her? Dating in the twenty-first century is hard enough, they say, and hard-to-please women like her only make things worse.

"At least he calls instead of texts all the time," her women friends say. "You're lucky. Don't be such a diva!"

"If a guy doesn't call, it's a problem. If he calls too much, it's a problem," her male friends say. "You women are never satisfied."

They dub her "high maintenance" before they unfriend her and vanish from her social media feed, claiming that she's the prime example of what's wrong with the current dating scene—today's black woman wants too much. In a world where men and women ghost one another all the time, cutting off communication without warning or reason, she should be grateful he bothers to call and honored to meet his family. As long as he doesn't flood her inbox with pictures of his penis, she should thank her lucky stars.

How could she guess that the bar had fallen so low? How could she predict that eating with a man in a public restaurant would seal the deal, committing her to a long-distance relationship with a man she's never even kissed? How can she possibly see this far ahead when there are candles on the table and crisp linen napkins and couples all around them, and simply sitting there and taking it in is all she wants to do? Grateful to sit still after a flurry of professional activities, she's just glad for the chance to sip her wine, to sit back in her seat, and to enjoy the pleasure of eating without having to rush off to the next thing. For her, this dinner is a much-needed break, a respite from the whirl. How can she guess that, to him, this meal means much, much more?

Later that night, back in her hotel room, she surfs the cable channels she doesn't have at home, coming across a marathon for a show called *Catfish* that calls to mind an old white-haired man with a Cajun accent and a cooking show her mother watched long ago on PBS. Instead of learning the proper ways to blacken or fry catfish, she gets a reality show about online daters so desperate that they fall in love with strangers, baring their hearts and souls to people they've never met in person, whose faces they've never seen, and whose identities they cannot confirm. She watches two white men supersleuths help the lovelorn put real faces to fake profiles, and she waits for the punch line, but there's nothing funny about these hopefuls who latch on so quickly and attempt to build on so little. She feels so out of touch, like one who has been asleep for a millennium, awakening to a world where love is founded upon the frequency rather than the substance of communication and where calling every day matters more than what is actually said.

But, now, sitting across from him in this restaurant, she's neither heard of nor seen *Catfish*, so she knows it only as a bottom-feeding fish that pairs well with hush puppies, so she has no inkling that people are so eager for relationships and so desperate for love that they will peer into a drop of water and see an entire ocean, so she doesn't know to be wary, so when he picks up the check at the end of the meal and says he's had a wonderful evening and asks her if it would be all right for him to call her sometime, she sees no harm at all in agreeing.

"Sure," she says. "Why not?"

Come Sunday

ome Sunday, William thinks better of it all but doesn't know how to say so.

Lying beside him the night before, Natalie had said, "Sometimes I get the feeling that you don't actually like me. It's as if there's something about me that just rubs you the wrong way."

"It's too late for this kind of discussion. I need to sleep," William had said, though they both knew he'd napped the afternoon and early evening away. "We'll talk later."

"You show your friends a patience I never seem to get from you."

"They need it."

She'd shifted away from him, and the covers had gone with her, leaving him cold and exposed. "And I don't? What about me?"

"It's really late," he'd said.

"I'm not going to feel better until I can get this off my chest," she said.

"Later," he yawned loudly, lacing his fingers behind his head underneath the pillow.

Soon after, he felt her leave the bed. Several minutes later, the front door closed. After she'd gone, he'd gotten up to check. Her car keys dangled from their hook. It was too late and too dangerous for her to be taking a walk this time of night by herself, William thought. It was a ploy to get him to come after her, to force him to talk.

He turned the lights off and got back into bed.

Come Sunday, he awakens to noise. There are two women in his living room, helping Natalie pack. They have boxes, fat rolls of brown tape, tall nonfat lattes, and crumbly scones. One braces herself against a box to hold its flaps tightly together while zipping a fat piece of tape straight down the middle and ripping it off against the metal teeth of the dispenser. The other woman packs elephant figurines from Natalie's sorority days, swathing each one in newspaper to prevent breakage.

The women are not actually noisy. It is the sucking sound of tape being pulled off its dispenser, the sliding of boxes along the floor, the stacking of them on a hand truck against the wall by the front door—it is the sound of their efficiency that has jarred him awake.

Natalie directs them from the center of the room. William clears his throat and she raises red and sleepless eyes to him. She looks where he is looking, at the large, framed painting on the wall above the sofa.

For a moment, he hopes she is remembering what he remembers.

William had bought the painting for her after she'd dragged him to one of her sorority functions, a jazz brunch for which he'd had to wear formal attire. Out of place in a room filled mostly with women, he'd stayed by her side while she greeted one sorority sister after another, until his head swam with introductions and he began to feel less like a boyfriend and more like an appendage. Excusing himself to the mimosa fountain, he'd wandered the perimeter of the room, perusing the items displayed for silent auction. William was debating whether to write a bid on a basketball autographed by John Starks when he saw the painting on the wall.

In it, a woman emerges out of a collage. Head tilted, she gazes inquisitively at someone out of the frame. Standing on her front porch, she looks at the person as though to ask him to state his purpose. Hands wrapped around a weathered brown pole staked into the ground, in the space of her arms she cradles a small child. One hand only on his ankles, she balances him easily, effortlessly, as if dropping him is an impossibility not to be borne. So sure and self-contained despite the precariousness of the child in her arms, despite the poor quality of her clothing, despite the bandanna tied around her head, despite the adult and child some distance behind her, walking away, she seems to say that she is the only one not in need of tending. The brown pole she clasps is striped with white lines, which could be either the pale wood beneath the bark or the effects of chipping, flaking, rusting metal. Yet it is the pole—and only the pole—that is in disrepair. She and hers are fine, or soon will be.

The woman in the collage made him think of Natalie, though it wasn't the kind of artwork he could be sure she would like. There was the possibility that she would be insulted. One look at the bandanna and she'd think of Aunt Jemima. How to say to her that the woman was her? How to let her know that they both gave off that same sense of immense capability? Maybe Natalie would not care for it, but he'd liked it nonetheless. The way the artist had put the woman together out of bits and pieces, of shapes, colors, and prints, made him think of quilts, of the patchwork quality of life, of the way his mother had spent her life gathering scraps and fusing them into something meaningful for him and his brother, of the way, generations before, grandmothers and great-aunts had collected the castaways of others and sewn together bits and pieces of fabric to create both beauty and warmth from scraps.

William had signed his name on the bidding sheet and checked the list every fifteen minutes to see if anyone had outbid him. By the jazz brunch's end, he'd paid more than he'd intended to, but he'd bought the painting for her and would be able to hang it and look at it whenever he liked.

"What about that?" he asks, wanting the painting to make her stay.

She says, "I'll come back for it tomorrow."

The next day, William calls in sick. He wants to be there when Natalie comes for the painting.

His doorbell rings midafternoon, and he rushes to open it. Before him stands a man in blue, holding a clipboard. "Good afternoon, sir. Are you happy with your cable television provider?" the salesman asks.

"No, I'm not happy at all," William admits.

"Would you be interested in talking over your options to see if we can't do something about that?"

"I would love to talk," William says.

William ushers the salesman into the foyer, where they stand awkwardly. The salesman launches into an explanation about the new improvements that have been made and lists the cost-effectiveness of switching to another carrier. He suggests the practicality of bundling services for even further savings.

"How does that sound, sir?" the salesman asks him.

"It's so hard to know what to do."

"There's a thirty-day guarantee," the salesman says. "If you change your mind, you'll only be charged the onetime installation fee. After that you're off the hook. We'll retrieve our materials and it will be as if they never were." The salesman snaps his fingers.

As the salesman takes down his information and directs him to the appropriate places to sign, William wishes it were that easy. Removal, indifference, upheaval all took work and required effort. One had to pretend the loss was minuscule. And it didn't matter if you kept silent, ignored it, willed it away, or pretended everything was fine and that nothing needed saying. Silence would not save you. The loss would still come and linger and make it so you felt you could never escape it. He'd had a chance to speak, to say something that would have made things right. He could have gone after her two nights ago. He should have, for the sake of her safety. Instead he'd acted like a boy in grade school, showing affection through meanness, substituting cruelty for love.

After William signs the last document, the salesman rises from the couch, smiles widely, and tucks his clipboard under his arm. "Well sir, I guess that will be all."

"Wait."

"Yes?"

William turns from the salesman to the wall behind him. He crawls onto the couch and lifts the painting from the wall. It slides into his hands, heavy and solid. He grips the canvas in both hands and thrusts it at the salesman.

"Yours if you want it," he says to the salesman, who can only stare, at a loss for words.

Childhood, Princesshood, Motherhood

She wants to return the presents with notes of apology that say: *No princesses allowed.* Her husband says they can accept the gifts and toss them or pass them on to others. But it's not just one gift. At the baby shower, she receives a passel of bow-wrapped bundles of white or pale pink onesies and bibs that say MOMMY'S LITTLE PRINCESS or DADDY'S LITTLE PRINCESS. The ones that say neither say BAD TO THE BOW.

She wants to stop the princess tide now, before it's too late.

He says what's done is done. Hasn't she ever wanted to be a princess?

Back when the only princess that mattered was Luke's twin, Leia—when princesses shot blasters, withstood Imperial probes, bluffed generals, disguised themselves as bounty hunters to threaten giant slugs with thermal detonators—a princess seemed like a pretty good thing to be. But that was before playing dress-up moved from the house and took to the streets and little girls sat in the McDonald's in tiaras, tutus, and glitter face paint, before everything—even Legos—got segregated into pink or blue and she swore off having children.

She'd changed her mind about *that*, he's quick to remind her.

Though she finds parenthood palatable with him at her side, she is still sickened by the current child-worshiping cult-trend.

Just the thought of being known only as someone's mom, replacing her political candidate's bumper sticker with one about honor roll status, synchronizing snacks and playdates, carrying EpiPens, offering trick-or-treat snacks to account for every allergy, living a juice-box-ready life, and planning themed birthday parties because cakes made from boxes no longer cut it kept her backing away from every child she saw as if one touch from their grubby, germy, snotty hands could turn her into a mother.

But she has him, and they've agreed to do it their way, to make their own rules and not cave in to the pressure, to parent as they see fit.

Is he copping out on her now, before they even begin?

Of course not, but he thought the onesies were cute. He didn't really see the harm.

She asks if he remembers his last girlfriend.

How could he forget? Spoiled rotten to the core, she'd taken every courtesy as her due, acting as if he lived only to serve her. She never thanked him for opening her doors, never once offered to pay for a date, not even on his birthday. She'd wanted a wedding whose dress alone would have cost more than his current home's down payment.

She points to the bedazzled onesies and bibs, asks where he thinks that behavior comes from. How does he think it all begins?

If he were a cartoon, above his head would appear a light bulb. He gathers up the onesies and the bibs, snatches the cards right out of her hands. He agrees, they must send it all back. *No princesses allowed.* He volunteers to write the notes himself.

Hunger Memory

The question comes from somewhere over her right shoulder, where the server stands just out of view but close enough to take her order. *What will you have?*

What she wants and what she will have are never quite the same. Always, they will be two different things. Right now she craves a slice of cheese melted over a piece of bread that has been broiled in the oven, and she wants it slightly overdone so that the edges where the cheese meets the bread are browned, so that the cheese makes a bubble in the center—wanting it the way she'd learned to make it for herself during those long-ago late afternoons when she let herself in with a latchkey and waited for someone to come home and take care of her so she could be done looking after herself.

She cannot have that at a place like this. Only the very poor still make toast that way, broiling it in an oven, using one appliance in place of two. Everyone else uses a toaster. How she hates it the new middle-class way—the dry offering of toaster-toasted bread, the awful way the bread resists the butter, that grating sound of the knife scraping against it, more irritating to her than nails on a chalkboard, and worst of all, the way the toast flakes when buttered, leaving crumbs, disgusting little pieces of itself, all over the table.

She feeds on her memory of hunger while the server waits. *Ma'am? Do you need a few more minutes to look over the items?*

She opens the menu and orders half a grapefruit, the first item she sees.

When it comes, she digs in with her spoon. Lifting a ruby-red section, she carries it to her lips. On her tongue it tastes sour as poverty, bitter as life.

Howl

I called my mother this morning, speaking in growls and roars. She cut me off right away. "Can't speak Wolf right now. I just finished making breakfast. Call you back in five."

Wolfspeak was for when the bottom fell out of words, so she knew it was important. Five minutes later she called back, guessing there had been a breakup. She said, "You should have seen this coming. Even a blind man could."

He said he saw a future with me and then walked me through his town house so I could see it too. Upstairs he showed me the bedrooms. We'd sleep in the first one, and since the second was his home office, I assumed the third would become mine. He said, "No, we'll save that one for children," and led me downstairs where my office awaited—it looked just like a kitchen table. I was to work there on nonteaching days, grading papers while watching kids. Gloating about the money we'd save on childcare, he said this was the perk of being with a professor. Anyone could have seen it coming. Anyone but me.

I told my mother in my own way, whimpers and howls explaining how it all went down. How he saw me as more womb than woman. How I almost didn't walk away. How leaving him had been touch and go. How I'd gone into it for love and nearly settled for erasure. How for this there were no words and only howling would do.

The Best That You Can Do

hey caught a cab after a late evening in Olde City, and as the cab turned off of Market and took Walnut— she wanted to pass the theaters—she leaned her head back against his arm and said, "I used to love doing this when I lived in Manhattan, taking cab rides the long way home, just so I could see the streetlights going by in my window. Ivan called me a spendthrift, but I saved on other things to be able to do it when I wanted."

"Ivan?"

"Don't you remember Ivan? I told you about him before."

He remembered mention of an Ivan who'd been a part of her cohort in graduate school, not an Ivan who'd taken scenic cab rides with her. Not an Ivan spoken of in the way one speaks of one who has formerly been a lover.

"Didn't you go to school with him?"

"You do remember. He dropped out, though."

She opened her window to let the air in. She kept her eyes closed and rolled her head to the side closer to him.

When they'd gotten into the cab, the theme song from *Arthur* had been on the radio before she'd closed the partition to block out the cabbie's cell phone. He'd never liked that movie but he'd always liked the song, although he didn't understand the part about being caught between the moon and New York City. He figured it was because he was from Philadelphia and not New York. He figured it was an insider thing. It was probable that Ivan knew what that part meant. It was possible that Ivan knew much, much more.

Ivan would not care for the weight of her head numbing his arm to sleep either. Sitting beside her in the cab, Ivan would nonchalantly shake her off his arm. When she began to complain, he'd trail his fingertips over her collarbone, then maybe undo the first few buttons of her lacy blouse and open her top just low enough for the cabbie to wonder.

Ivan would know exactly when to stop. He'd know she was curiously excited beside him. He'd tug the pendant on her necklace—a tiny, gold four-leaf clover—tug and slide it across the chain until it rested high on her neck, near enough for him to lean over her and take it into his mouth. The cabbie, imagining more, would never know the difference while Ivan tasted the metal and the salt from her skin. As he did it, Ivan would know he'd just made a memory that she would one day blurt on a cab ride with a newer boyfriend. Ivan would know that the newer guy would believe her when she said he was a friend from grad school in town for a couple of days crashing on her couch. Knowing all of this, Ivan would not only humor her request to have the cab take them the long way home, but he'd tip the cabbie double.

Diminishing Returns

No matter how hard you try, the more you give, the more it takes.

Each additional unit of effort yields less and less. Dinners, painstakingly cooked after watching hours of *Emeril* and *Barefoot Contessa*, do not bring him home earlier, nor do they convince him to stop working late. Hours of kettlebell reps, spin classes, and Pilates have produced a firm, flexible, and defined body that does not draw him closer at night. There is less of an aggregate demand for you. In fact, there is no demand at all for the services you supply.

It used to take only a look, a word, a spritz of perfume, a strap off the shoulder, a hook come undone. You keep making the effort, but there is no return on your investment. Close your eyes. See his love mapped out on a pie chart? No, not a pie chart. A linear trend graph. See how that thick black line inches lower and lower? Each notch on the x-axis is a year of your marriage. See how the line angles down, sliding like an avalanche until it runs off the bottom of the page? That's this year.

Foolishly, you speculated, believing you had invested wisely, believing love could grow and mature risk-free.

You should have known better. After Enron. After Martha

Stewart went to jail. After the levees in Louisiana. After the collapses of banks. After checked baggage fees. After oil spills on the Gulf Coast. After earthquakes in Haiti. After floods in Tennessee.

Fool to believe that the world as you know it could change right before your eyes and love—somehow—maintain its solvency. The market is a vehicle of risk; love is not FDIC insured.

A Recipe for Curry

CHICKEN CURRY
*Serve with roti for a satisfying supper the
entire family can enjoy!*

One pound chicken
Potatoes, peeled and quartered
Curry paste
Cumin
One onion, chopped
Two cloves garlic, finely chopped
Pepper
Water
Salt to taste

A fire kept low. A firm grasp. A tilt of the handle spreads the oil so it can heat evenly as it coats the bottom of the pan.

The ingredients are all laid out. All within her reach. She adds a handful of chopped garlic, watching as the small white slivers dance upon contact with the hot oil. She stirs it to keep it from sticking to the pan. As soon as the slivers start to brown, she adds her pile of chopped onions and sautés them until they are soft and tender.

Liliane is making curry.

With a large sharp knife, she slowly pulls chicken away from the bone until her bowl is filled with cut pieces of the meat.

She hates making this dish. But Selwhyne wants it once a week. To remind him, he says. To help him remember.

But you don't need to be reminded, she has told him more than once. Your mind, your heart, your tongue can never forget. When you close your eyes at night, you go back to Guyana, back to Georgetown when you dream. Your tongue refuses to forget the flavor of your home. So how can you ever forget?

He doesn't listen. Once a week he wants curry and roti. Chicken curry. Lamb curry. Shrimp curry. She is sick of curry.

And he is growing older and fatter and more stubborn by the day. His face has darkened with age. No longer the mellow color of hominy but now more like the pinch of cumin she adds at the end to give the spicy sauce some color. He has forgotten all the things they were supposed to do once they got to the United States.

In Guyana, the legend says that if you eat labba and drink creek water you are a native son, a native daughter. That you are bound to come back. Selwhyne's aunt had cooked labba curry for them on their last night in Georgetown, and they'd been forced to band together and use their wiles to avoid eating it. They had sat side by side, giddy with their plans and determination, wondering how they would get through the meal without offending. They had been co-conspirators that night, partners, a couple. They had already agreed that they didn't want to return. Not now with Burnham in charge, everything nationalized, and inflation up high enough to be laughable. There would be nothing to return to. In leaving Guyana, they were following the crowd. All the civil servants, the people who wanted to protect what little money they already had and watch it grow, were leaving in droves. Those who could afford to leave were not waiting around. And she and Selwhyne were joining them. Neither she nor Selwhyne considered themselves to be superstitious, but they didn't want to return once they left and they weren't taking any chances. They refused to let tradition interfere with their plans.

Selwhyne's aunt had urged her to try the dish. So Liliane had taken a small bite of the curry, to appease. Slyly, she concealed the morsel between her gum and cheek; she had no intention of actually eating it. Selwhyne put a warning hand on her knee. "Don't swallow," he whispered to her as they sat side by side and listened to his aunt, his nearness more potent to her than his words. She did not see how they were to avoid it, but she had not been brought up to question others with food in her mouth. "It will come to us," he reassured her, patting her knee, leaving a spot of warmth where his palm lingered. "We'll figure out how to get out of this." Back then, she had still been intoxicated by the smell of his aftershave clinging to his chin, still fascinated by the way his mustache twitched back and forth above his upper lip when he spoke to her. She nodded and shifted the morsel from the side of her cheek to the underside of her tongue and allowed the morsel to liquefy while she waited.

Selwhyne's aunt smiled at their whispers and made remarks about newlyweds and youthful brides. Then she excused herself and went to the kitchen to fetch a pitcher of water to give them a moment of privacy. Once Selwhyne's aunt was gone, Liliane spat her food into her dinner napkin.

"Your purse," Selwhyne said. "We'll stow it there."

They transferred her purse's contents to his pockets. "Make haste," he urged, as they scraped labba curry into their dinner napkins—their knees bumping each other in their hurry—and stuffed them into her purse. Selwhyne arranged the remainder of food on their plates with an artist's precision, camouflaging portions of the labba curry underneath ripped-off pieces of flat roti bread. Liliane scraped off enough into the napkins to make it look as though they had been eating steadily in his aunt's absence, but she made sure to leave enough in plain view on their plates to show that they were not gluttonous.

They had been so young then.

She was a young girl and Selwhyne was distinguished, an educator by trade. When they reached New York, Selwhyne would go to graduate school in order to qualify to do research at a prestigious university. And there would be plenty of opportunities for her as well. Selwhyne assured her of it. She wanted to teach elementary school and be surrounded by children every day. Selwhyne encouraged her in her hopes. There would be plenty of chances for her to be surrounded by children, not only her pupils but her own children as well. The ones she and Selwhyne would make and raise together, future professionals—doctors, nurses, scholars, and lawyers—that would make their parents proud. That night, their plans, their dreams, their hopes had been intertwined. So Liliane put her fate in her husband's hands. She did not swallow.

But that was long ago. Nothing worked out the way they planned. They never became different people. She had not been allowed to teach young American children. She was told that she needed to learn to speak English first. Guyana was the only country in South America that could boast English as its primary language. Now she was told that she couldn't speak it, that the children couldn't understand her language, which was the same as theirs. As time passed, Liliane refused to think of the denial. She learned not to look at herself. Instead, she focused on her husband and saw that Selwhyne was only becoming more and more the same with time. Nothing changed him. The same Old Spice he splashed on his face and neck as a young man when the skin from his chin to neck was so tight and supple that she could not pull enough of it between her teeth to give him a love bite. The same way of drinking his tea too strong, too hot. So hot he had to blow on it, then sip it quick between clenched teeth. The same way of wiping the corners of his mouth before and after eating, his dimpled fingers like tightly cased sausages dabbing at the edges of his mouth where his bottom and top lip converged. The same way of rubbing his lips together with his middle and index finger after kissing her. The same way of making love to her after all these years. As if they were still strangers.

The same promises. Next year. A house. Next year. A car. Next year, we will send for your brother. We should wait for children. Until we are stable. Until we have enough and can provide. Next year, maybe.

Long ago, she stopped keeping count. The only way she knew that one year was almost over was that Selwhyne began to talk about the next one.

Her fingernails are yellowed and caked with curry paste, which dries in the beds of her cuticles and stains her fingers. Before and after she cooks, she scrubs the undersides of her fingernails with a nail brush, but the stains still will not come out.

She mixes the curry paste with water in a small glass bowl, then spoons it out onto the pan, mixing it with the onions and garlic and oil. Now it is beginning to smell like something.

She adds the potatoes and slowly stirs in water to create a

sauce. The curry paste and water blend into a yellowish mixture that fills half the pan. The liquid is thin and runny, but it will thicken upon standing.

The raw pink flesh of chicken browns in a pan of curry. Her wooden spoon turns the chicken every other minute to make sure it browns and gets cooked all the way through. The sauce thickens over it. Soon the chicken and potatoes are the same dark yellow-brown of the curry. Onions disintegrate.

Liliane would sometimes slice a mango and add the chunks of it to the curry. Or she'd quarter a fat, juicy, red tomato and throw it in for color. Just for variety. Just to try something different. Now, she cannot remember the last time she varied her recipe. She, too, is still the same. The same girl from Georgetown. The same young woman who learned how to separate the man from his dreams, to accept and love them separately, for they were no longer connected. The same woman who decides each week in her kitchen that this will be the last time she makes him this dish, the last time she carries food to the table to watch him eat it without speaking to her. The same old woman who still serves him, dishing his food up and carrying it out to him even though there is nothing wrong with his hands. The same wife who watches as he wipes his mouth before eating and kissing, knowing that before the night is over, he will make love to her as if they are still strangers. Each week she decides that she will run away and leave him to make his own curry; threatens to water down the curry so that it is made the way they make it in U.S. West Indian restaurants, to burn the roti, to make her presence known. To tell him that they were supposed to become different people together but that she is still waiting for him.

She adds the cumin and the red pepper, watching as the spoonful of cumin darkens the mixture, tinting it. She stirs until she is sure it has mixed all through, until she can no longer see the red pepper flakes she has sprinkled in. When the thick sauce bubbles, she adds a pinch of salt. Then she lowers the flame under the pan and covers it and lets it simmer.

Now she has time to roll out the roti dough and make the flat flaky bread her people have inherited from the Indian laborers brought over on *The Whitby* and *Hesperus* to work in Guyana. Selwhyne took her to an Indian restaurant in Manhattan once. They had eaten from the buffet and she had piled the bread they called naan on her plate, but when she saw the way the other patrons were eating it, separately, not as a wrap for the food, she'd lost her appetite. She'd felt out of place, homesick and lost, unsure of how to eat the strange yet familiar bread, wondering how an almost identical food could serve such a different purpose.

A pinch of salt. Flour. And small spoonfuls of water. She can make the roti with her eyes closed. She needs only to feel the press of moist dough being molded into a ball beneath her fingertips and palms. She lines the balls of dough in front of the rolling pin like extra artillery waiting to be called into service. She sprinkles flour on the surface of the table to prevent the dough from sticking. She holds the rolling pin upended in one hand, coating it in flour with the other hand. She runs her hand up and down the length of it from its base to its smoothly rounded tip in slow smooth strokes.

She never used to have to coax him at night. Never had to work magic with her hands all over his body to make him respond. He used to reach for her.

Next year. A house. Next year. Things will all be different next year. Have patience.

Dough flattens beneath her rolling pin and she presses down

hard, gripping each end with force, pressing and rolling until the dough can't get any flatter.

Have patience. Next year. A house. Next year. A car. Things will all be different next year. You'll see.

Dough. Pressed flat. Next year. Rolled into paper thinness. Next year. A house. Next year. A car. Next year, things will be different for us. She heats the other skillet. Next year. The flat roti shrinks in the skillet; its edges pull in upon themselves. Next year. Different. Next year. Dough cakes and hardens under her fingernails, irritating the sensitive skin there, clinging. Next year. Next year. Patience. Next year. Next year. Next year.

A stack of warm roti cools under a damp cloth. Chicken curry sits in its pan, covered tightly. As always, she cleans up before she calls him for dinner. There will be no help from him. She knows what not to expect. So she takes a dishcloth and wipes the counter down. She prepares their plates and packs the rest of the meal away in airtight Tupperware containers. She fills the sink with warm soapy water and immerses the pans, measuring spoons, rolling pin, bowls, knives, and cutting boards into the water. She washes all the dishes and leaves them on the dish drainer to air-dry. Before she takes his plate out to the dining room, she tries once more to scrub the yellow stains out from beneath her fingernails.

But the stains will not come out.

Now she will sit and they will eat and she will listen to the promises all over once again. After dinner, when the dishes have dried, she will be careful—so careful—to put each pan and utensil back in its proper place. She needs to know exactly where to find them for next week, when she will once again prepare curry for his dinner.

Brat

The boy, facing backward in the seat before her, is enough to work a nerve. Staring at her—snotty-nosed, unkempt, and uncombed—he raps his knuckles against the back of his seat, tapping a loud beat in front of her, snaring her attention. She lowers her book, raises an eyebrow, scans the bus for a parent, an older sibling, someone—anyone—to claim and hush him. The seat beside him is empty. He is riding alone, unattended as can be.

If he would only stop.

He hangs over the back of his seat and beats his tune with the self-absorption of a gum smacker, a pencil tapper, a pen clicker—too pleased by the sounds of his own making to care about anyone else. She motions for him to face forward, but he ignores her. The more she frowns and motions, the harder he hits the seat and the wider he grins, declaring the concert is just for her.

No way to escape him. Save for the empty seat beside him, the bus is filled with all the passengers who crowded in at Sixty-Ninth Street Terminal. So she rides with his incessant thumping as the bus drives beside the golf course and passes the ShopRite. By the time the bus turns the corner in front of the CVS, she can take no more. She whispers, "Stop that right now. Turn around and behave."

The boy halts his rapping, flips her the bird, and returns to his obnoxious drumming.

Such an adult gesture in one so young—it catches her off guard. Was this the way it began—with the making of oneself into a public nuisance? Was she wrong to expect better from these children turned brats? Coddled by network channels, movies, and fast-food meals that all catered to them, they couldn't help but be filled with the importance of their own being. Now they were taking over, bombing high schools, beating men to death on subway platforms, committing flash robberies down on South Street, riding public transportation as if they owned it, taking seats reserved for the elderly and the disabled, littering their snacks, blaring their music, and jabbering on their cellular phones in illiterate and remedial tongues. Loud and rowdy, insolent and uncaring, they filled up buses and subways, sprawling, cursing like adults, refusing to make way for riders like herself who were tired and weary and burdened with jobs and bills and real-life worries, who simply wanted to read on the ride home.

Provoked beyond her limit, she wants to yank him across the seat and teach him a thing or two about courtesy, but instead she leans in close and mouths words for his ears only. The boy's hands still, his beating comes to an abrupt end. He turns and faces forward—quiet—seen but not heard for the rest of the ride.

She picks up her book. Smiling, she begins to read.

Minnow

When my doctor says the fetus is just a tiny sliver, a little minnow inside of me, I imagine myself a lake. It is a daunting task, keeping my minnow afloat, a full-time job. I no longer bother to revise my dissertation. Now I only pretend.

It is a task to sit through the weekly three-hour dissertation workshop. As others compare methodology sections and scholarly overviews, I excuse myself to the restroom, feeling only the needs of my bladder. When the seminar ends, I walk toward home down Walnut Street, stopping at the used bookstore on Fortieth Street to visit the cats.

Previously, the bookstore had been the Philly Diner, and Tim and I used to go in for cheesesteaks. Now that he has moved in, we never go anywhere together, and I come alone. If I browse long enough, one or both of the two neutered toms—heavy and fat with low-hanging bellies—will find me. Before we discovered Tim's allergy, I'd had a platinum Burmese named Ash. This moment of feline infidelity—when the cats come to me, a stranger, and rub against my calves and shins—is the one I crave. Their warm fat bodies fill me with hope. As I kneel to pet them, I feel the minnow within me coming to life.

At home, Tim and I watch the latest news on the Philadelphia "serial cat killer." Four dead cats are found in Kensington, beaten to death or impaled through the mouth with a stick, their bodies too tortured for viewers to see. Although it is not morning, bile rises to my throat, and I can't keep it in. I throw up in the space between the TV and my feet, with Tim on the couch beside me. This is not the first time, but it is not until now that Tim puts two and two together and understands what it has all been about.

He returns with paper towels, disinfectant spray, a sponge, and a plastic bucket of soapy water. He hands me a damp paper towel to wipe my mouth. He pulls on yellow plastic gloves and kneels to clean my mess. Scrubbing, he looks at me, eyes accusing. "Why didn't you tell me?"

Because it's mine, I think to say. My body has just become ours. No longer my own little minnow swimming inside the lake that is me. Now there is a rowboat on my lake, an oar cutting through, a fisherman trying to catch my elusive, slippery, silvery minnow.

I refuse the paper towel, wiping my mouth instead with the back of my hand. "Let me," I say, taking the bucket and sponge from him. "I'll do it." Kneeling beside him, I strip him of his gloves, wanting to clean the mess myself, wanting to finish this task first, before rinsing my mouth and brushing my teeth, knowing that after the mess I have made of things, it will be the last decision I will make alone.

Second Sally

The year was new, rife with the smell of door fronts freshly cleared of snow and lives swept clean, stark as the withered bushes in her apartment complex's courtyard whose gnarled naked branches snagged her on her way to work. This year she resolved to slip loose the predictable knot that yoked her, to be seen, to make them know her name. Back home people had at least taken the time to make the inevitable bad jokes. When her parents first took off her training wheels, they'd cheered, "Ride, Sally, ride," as she wobbled on her bicycle down the street. When she matured, boys joked that they would never tell her to slow her mustang down. But that was a different world, a different time, a different place. She'd left the old Sally behind and had come to Chicago to be rebuilt as the city itself had been rebuilt, to be a Second Sally in Second City. Now she lived along the shore of a lake in a flat land, in an architect's dream of a city, a city of renewal, sprung from the ashes of that great fire long ago. Here, now, in the here and now, no one brought up Wilson Pickett or Lou Reed songs and cracked jokes—no one cared enough to tease. Here, she'd traded scrutiny for invisibility, but there was time to change all of that. The year was brand-new and there was time enough, time for anything.

Doing It

"Lights out. All freshmen in bed." Kaminsky raps on the door. His feet are a shadow just outside the dorm room's door. "Get to bed. Now."

Paul walks over to the light switch and flicks it off. It is on Jay's side of the room, near the head of the bed, where Jay has Maria smuggled beneath the covers. The light goes out and Kaminsky's feet disappear. Paul can hear Kaminsky plod past 324, which he skips since Shaun is a senior. Paul hears Kaminsky patter across the hall to 325. Jacob and Hadav's room. "Lights out."

With visiting hours and study hall both over, Maria should be back in her own room, back in her own dorm, but instead Jay and Maria are in Jay's bed, doing it. Squeezed against the wall and huddled under the thin navy blue blanket, they writhe. Jay's elbows poke the sheet upward. He covers Maria's mouth to keep her from crying out. One of Maria's feet hangs out, dangling below the edge of the blanket. It thumps the side of the mattress, keeping time with her muffled groans.

They do it twice a week, except when it's Maria's time and she won't. Jay is one lucky bastard.

Maria is almost there. Her foot stops thumping against the bed. Now it is digging into the bed's side so she can push upward.

Paul looks. Her brown calf grazes the side of the bed, and her foot digs in like a stirrup, like the bed is her horse. Paul is her horse, and she is not too heavy for him. Her foot does not hurt him. It feels good. It is a command to him: go faster. It is a reminder: look, I am still here. It is a gauge: I'm on my way, I'm coming, I'm there, I'm gone.

Maria jumps, startled. She hears the noise. She hears Paul. She peeks out from the covers and looks to Paul's side of the room; her foot bounces against the bed.

Slip

My grandmother slipped out of her skin and became a young girl once again.

I saw her as I never knew her, as only pictures could tell, a young girl with eyes bright and teeth just a few, a girl who knew nothing of the life that was coming.

Slipped from her skin, she became slick as an eel. In her hands she held a buttery ear of corn. Missing her two front teeth she yet went to town on the cob, eating straight across before on to the next row of kernels, her delight the small, delicious bell of a typewriter's carriage returning.

My grandmother slipped out of her skin and a new young girl emerged, grasping a piece of chalk. She knelt and drew a hopscotch court; she jumped and skipped in the boxes; she hopped on one leg.

My grandmother slipped out of her skin and out came a blossom of a girl, all petal, all flower, a woman young and in love. She laughed and her laughter caught the question on the breeze and blew back an answer—*yes*.

My grandmother slipped out of her skin and into her Sunday best. She lined up her three children outside the church's black gates—two little men in black suits standing on either side of my mother as they waited for the car that was to take them where they had to go. In that decade for widowhood—Myrlie, Betty, Coretta—my grandmother slipped past notice. Only the wind knew what she'd lost. The breeze disturbed her coiffure, whipped her hair all over, blew an apology of strands across her eyes—*sorry for your loss.*

Each time my grandmother slipped out of her skin, it was just long enough for a body to breathe, but still I held my breath, wondering how long before the skin became too tight, too taut, with all it must absorb. Skin, they say, renews itself, new cells replacing the old everywhere but in the brain—those burrowing, bruising memories are for a lifetime, forever hers to keep. When she slipped from her skin it stood there empty, just a husk, patiently waiting, though we both knew the future was no lure. It was love that always called her back, ensuring her return. And love—isn't it a burden, heavier than a satchel slung over the shoulder carrying a thousand lifetimes, a thousand memories, a thousand skins?

My grandmother slipped out of her skin, and as it stood there empty, I stepped in.

In the Name of Love

He is all apology when he calls her from the office to say he's got to work late. Something has come up—it can't be helped. A new project of the utmost importance. In fact, he'll have to work late for the next few nights, possibly even for the next few weeks, until his team meets their deadline. He is the soul of contriteness as he breaks the news to her. He's so sorry to spring it on her like this, so last minute. He knows that it's his night to cook.

She turns down her car's stereo, where she's been listening to a greatest hits compilation CD of Diana Ross and the Supremes. She'll swap chores with him for as long as he needs. She'll cook each night if he'll man the dishes. All he's got to do is load and run the dishwasher each night whenever he gets in.

It doesn't seem fair, he says. It's nowhere near an even exchange; it's so very little of her to ask. Maybe he can also take over the laundry? Since it can be done any time of the day, it won't matter how late he gets in. Just think! She can wake up each morning to clean and folded clothing without having to scrub the dirt from his collars. After all, she's being so reasonable, so accommodating. It's the least he can do to carry his weight. He'll make it up to her, he promises. Just as soon as this project is complete, he'll take off a few days and they'll go somewhere nice, just the two of them. He's so glad that she's taking it all in stride, that she's not angry. It's just one of the reasons he loves her. Before he signs off, he reminds her not to wait up and says how lucky he is to have her. She is indeed the very best of wives; she's so very understanding.

Yes, she understands too well. This is not the first time he's had to "work late." Four years ago, that had been his excuse for six months straight before she'd ferreted out the truth and uncovered his affair. It had taken months of counseling to save their marriage. Fool that she was, she'd actually believed that they had come out stronger than before, that the counseling had opened lines of communication that time and habit had fused shut, that the affair had been the jolt their marriage had needed to shock them into a new awareness of each other, that they now worked harder to preserve what they had, now that they understood how fragile love was, how it could wither on a vine and die without constant nurturing. She'd imagined their therapist as a gardener with pruning shears, deadheading their relationship to promote rebloom.

She signals a turn that will take her to the supermarket instead of home. She leaves the stereo's volume turned low—the Supremes are now the last thing she wants to hear. All those songs of women waiting for their husbands to come to their senses, to stop in the name of love and come see about them while they wonder where their love went and when their men would be back in their arms again. In the silence left by the music, she hears the voices of her mother and aunts and the voices of her grandmother and great-aunts—the voices of the ages, the voices of generations of women who depended upon men for their happiness, who, like roses on a trellis, wound and looped and intertwined their lives over and around a man, relying on him for support and expecting him to hold them up. She can hear them all, all the voices of these women with their old-fashioned advice and well-worn adages about catching more flies with honey than vinegar, being vigilant about maintaining one's figure, and that the way to a man's heart is through his stomach. What did they know? Beyoncé. Halle Berry. Janet Jackson. Even Coretta Scott King, and she had been married to a man of God. Women who were far more accomplished and far more lovely than she had not been able to keep their partners from straying. Clearly, there was no formula, no set of behaviors, no insurance policy that could guarantee fidelity. She doesn't want hackneyed advice. She doesn't want a divorce and she doesn't want more counseling. She wants to not have to go through this all over again. All she wants is for this new affair to end as quickly as it can and to be the last of its kind. She wants her marriage to be hers.

The voices grow louder and louder until she's desperate enough to pull her hands from the steering wheel and cup them over her ears, and just then the ShopRite comes into view. She pulls into the parking lot and turns off the near-silent stereo; the women's voices clamor to make her listen, insisting they know just what she should do.

After six weeks of working late, he declares the project complete. He comes home just in time for dinner. She sets an extra place at the table so they can eat together again—finally. When she pulls the lasagna from the stove and carefully sets it down on the waiting trivet, the sharp smell of tomato and the creamy scent of ricotta waft into the air, filling his nose with tempting rich good-ness. The lasagna is piping hot, its top layers of cheese and sauce still bubbling; he wants nothing more than to dig right in, but she says that they must wait and let the dish rest for fifteen minutes. If they cut into the lasagna now it will fall apart. He's sorry to be so greedy. It seems that lately he's developed quite the appetite.

To pass the time she asks about the project. Has it been completed to his satisfaction, or does he anticipate more late nights? No, he assures her that project is over and done. She is surprised at how quickly it's come to an end. So is he; he'd thought it would last at least twice as long, but he's glad that it's all over. The last week had been stressful and full of infighting, accusations, and ridiculous expectations. He was glad to wash his hands of it—she knew how uncomfortable arguments made him. Maybe the next time something came up he'd tell them to pick a younger guy to head the project. He was older now and he didn't have the patience for drama. He would rather be at home with her. Working all those late nights had made him view her and their relationship in a different light. He was not a young man, and the things that used to excite him no longer held sway. Instead of dealing with unsupported complaints, unreasonable requests, and insufferable tantrums, he could have been here with her eating under the soft glow of their kitchen's light and enjoying evenings of repose.

She cuts the lasagna into generous portions and uses a spatula to transfer the squares onto their plates.

After he's had seconds he proposes a short trip, just the two of them. They can take off a Friday and its following Monday and make a long weekend of it.

She suggests somewhere warm and tropical. Sun, sand, beach.

He's thinking more along the lines of a hideaway in the mountains, a snug lover's cabin, where he can build them a fire and they can snuggle on the couch and . . . watch the flames. She might not have noticed, but he's put on a few pounds, what with all the late nights, and he has no desire to don swim trunks. No beach for him. There've been a few well-meaning jokes around the office about his new spare tire. What can he say? He'd loved her cooking. He tells her what all the dinners have meant to him, how he would come in at night so famished from all the work he had put in and see the foil-covered dish on the kitchen table or the pots on the stove and he'd just dig right in. Each night she'd prepared his favorites. Lasagna, smothered pork chops and baked macaroni and mashed potatoes, chicken parmigiana, baked ziti—so many saucy, cheesy, pasta dishes! And could he dare say no to her desserts? Caramel cake, sweet potato pie, banana pudding, peach cobbler—each night was like Thanksgiving come early. He couldn't help being greedy. He knew that he was supposed to apportion the meals and save some for leftovers the next night, but each night he'd finish whatever she had left out for him. After all, he hadn't wanted to appear ungrateful and offend her, or have her think he didn't appreciate all she did for him. He is so lucky to have her; she's been so very understanding.

She is indeed the very best of wives.

Prone

From some corner of the parking lot, Lucille is being watched. She does not know this—cannot know this—as she is preoccupied with gifts she has purchased for people who do not think of her at all. The bags she carries are not a struggle. No unwieldy double-tied, long-handled plastic bags with the ends of baseball bats or lacrosse sticks poking through. No colorful cardboard boxes with clear plastic fronts protecting dolls or action figures. No stuffed animals or lifelike babies who will feed or wet themselves upon command. No video simulations of football, baseball, or basketball for children too fat and lazy to play the actual sports themselves. She has purchased no toys, no gifts for children. From the corner where she is being watched—yes, even from there—it is easy to tell that she is not a mother or even anyone's favorite aunt.

No electronic gadgets for adult males, no sporting gear, no hardware tools among her purchases. Lucille has no lover.

No rectangular boxes of shoes. No tissue-wrapped purses. No cosmetics or perfumes. No free gift with purchase. Lucille is not vain.

Her packages are small. They fit into gift bags. Generic ties in muted colors. Fuzzy plush socks. Dancing Santa Clauses.

Ornamental picture frames. A matching set of wineglasses. A tin of powdered cocoa from Godiva. Gifts for coworkers, colleagues, bosses, Secret Santas and Hanukkah Harrys, people with whom she has no intimacy, people who will not miss her presence until something from her is needed. The gifts are gender-specific. Other than that, they are interchangeable. She will fill out the same note on each gift tag, writing simply: *For you.*

The lot is nearly empty now, the sort of setting people forward emails about, warning women to take caution. This is the time to enter by the passenger's side, the time not to linger as Lucille does, fussing with her bags in the back seat, arranging and rearranging before entering by way of the driver's side, squeezing past the car parked beside her, edging her in.

Lucille does not know any better. Statistics—she believes—made her safe. This—she thinks dimly—is the kind of thing that happens mostly to white women. They were the ones most prone, the ones usually grabbed in parking lots or stabbed while jogging late at night alone through darkened parks where no one had any business jogging in the first place. They were the ones dropped off at sides of the road, dumped in ditches or ravines, their bones and limbs bagged and burned. They were not her. Statistics kept her safe, made her less prone. Lucille knows she does not fit the profile, just as she knows her dark skin safeguards her from osteoporosis and reduces her risk of skin cancer, so she pays no heed to the man who suddenly emerges from his passenger's side, getting out of his car just as she is getting into hers.

Value Judgments

He thinks it's because of the miles between you. Five thousand miles round-trip between Philadelphia and San Francisco. Five hours and forty-seven minutes of peril—you always say your prayers before you get on and off the plane—yet you still kick off your shoes and place them under the seat in front of you.

But it's not the miles, or the three-hour time difference that always makes you too tired to do anything once you arrive, even though he's ready to paint the town. Miles and fatigue are as nothing to one who loves.

It's something else entirely that you cannot name.

An inflection, a slight lull on the phone when you mention coming to see him once your vacation starts in June, a chill that is his voice squeezed through the wires at MCI's rate of five cents per minute after 7:00 p.m., which erupts into "Well, I won't be able to pay for you the next time you come." You recover from feeling as if you'd just been slapped and murmur, "I didn't ask you to pay. And I didn't expect it." In your mind you have already hung up the phone and placed it gently down upon its receiver just so.

But you stay on the phone with him and arrange your trip in June. You tell him you'll try to get a nonstop flight.

Just before you hang up, you hear the confusion in his voice. You don't sound the same. Are you tired? Did he say something wrong? The back-and-forth of it all is getting to you, isn't it? But you understand why it must be you who makes the trips, don't you? He has an important job and he's only been there four months so he can't take vacation time just yet. He's in pharmaceuticals. He's saving the world or curing it. He is needed. You, you are only in graduate school and teaching English composition to college freshmen. You have all the time in the world. You can read your books on the plane. Just think. One more year.

You say nothing. He figures you are tired. He can understand that. Now he knows why you sound like you do.

But he does not.

He arrives at SFO on time, parks, and waits for you at baggage claim. Right away he recognizes your bag by its bright swirling Pepsi logo, a testimonial to all the hard work you put into collecting enough UPCs to earn the free duffel. Feeling magnanimous, he pulls it off the conveyor belt, grunting at how heavy it is. He thinks you have everything in here but the kitchen sink.

While he waits, he checks the name tag just to be sure it's really your bag. Squeezed onto the four tiny blue lines where an address is meant to go, he finds a message addressed to him. It says: *These belong to you.*

Pursed

Her change purse was always hungry, but today she had nothing to feed it. I'm hungry, it said, as if she couldn't tell. Its gold lips tarnished; its black body hollowed thin—she could see the signs for herself. Famished, it demanded to be fed. She slid her hands into the crevices of her couch but pulled up only dust. She shook the vacuum bag, hoping to hear the rattle of a coin. There's nothing here, she apologized. Anything, anything, the purse begged, mouth gaping open like the beak of a newborn bird awaiting its worm. I'm so sorry, she muttered, thinking of all she'd spent that day—on the dress; the books; her morning cortadito; her fare for the ride back home. The purse wheezed, its stomach full of air. Its mouth opened and closed repeatedly, making a clicking sound that drove her crazy. All right! she cried. There had to be something. The purse moaned, complaining of light-headedness. It said, I feel faint. She took it up in her arms and rocked it, cooing a lullaby. It curled against her breast and nuzzled. Its hunger-chapped lips closed around one of her blouse's dime-shaped buttons and tugged. Her blouse, delicate as all expensive things are, was not meant for such violence.

Another tug took the button right off—it fell into the abyss of the purse's mouth, leaving behind a lonely thread. She slapped the greedy mouth closed, quickly fastening its lips shut before it hungered for more.

Don't Mention It

What a long day. They are in bed, both tuckered out. Their daughter's asleep in her own room and everything in the house is calm and quiet. The only sounds are the little chuffing noises his wife makes just before falling into a deep sleep. She's beside him, burrowed beneath the covers, but he's wide-awake. He's thinking of the thing that's bothered him all evening.

He'd done his daughter's hair after dinner. While his wife cleared the table, he'd wrestled Hailey's thick hair into a semblance of order. Parting the kinky-coily mass down the center, fashioning a braid on each side of his daughter's head, and securing the ends of each braid with a colorful plastic barrette had made him feel like Michelangelo putting the finishing touches on the Sistine Chapel. He'd pulled out his cell phone and taken a few quick pictures of the top and back of his daughter's head to post on social media, careful not to show her face. When he'd proudly called attention to his handiwork, his wife had briefly looked up from where she stood at the kitchen sink and nodded before returning to the dinner dishes.

"Don't I even get a thank-you?" he'd blurted out, deflated.

With her back to him and her hands deep in suds she'd said, "Sweetie, don't forget to thank your father for doing your hair." His daughter had kissed his cheek wetly and said, "Thank you, Daddy," but her gratitude left him hollow.

The chuffing sounds grow louder. Five more minutes and his wife will be dead to the world. Falling asleep at the drop of a dime is her special talent.

He nudges her until she turns to him and pushes her satin eye mask onto her forehead. "What is it?"

"I didn't mean Hailey," he says.

She eyes him groggily and yawns into his face. "What?"

"Tonight, you told Hailey to thank me for doing her hair, but she wasn't who I meant."

His wife is wide-awake now. "So, you meant me?"

"Well," he says, "it was you I was doing the favor."

"Doing your own daughter's hair is not a favor to your wife."

He doesn't turn to her. He places his hands behind his head, finding it easier to say what needs to be said. "There are women who wish their husbands would help out around the house, but when I help, you don't even say thank you."

"Help?" She raises herself on an elbow to look down at him.

Suddenly, he feels sleepy. He closes his eyes. He can feel her staring, but he knows he's right. "They say men never help," he says. "Today I helped. Why shouldn't I be thanked?"

He opens an eye to see what she thinks. She's still looking at him queerly. "Thank you very much," she says. She slides her eye mask back down and huddles beneath their blankets once more.

"No problem," he says, pleased to be magnanimous. That's all he wanted. He is glad that he's stood his ground. He is glad that she understands.

———

The next morning is a horror. There is no breakfast when he comes downstairs. There's not even any coffee. His wife sits at their kitchen table with the morning paper, and his daughter concentrates on tying her shoelaces. "Slow start?" he asks.

"Hmm?" His wife doesn't look up. She's engrossed in the funnies.

"Where's breakfast?" he asks her.

"We've already had it," she says.

He looks to the sink where syrupy plates soak in soapy water. On the counter, the waffle iron is still smoking. "Where's mine?"

She shakes out the paper and turns the page, going from *Cathy* to *Blondie*. "You've never thanked me for making your breakfast, so today I didn't make any for you."

He's miffed that she's stooped to punishing him for last night, annoyed she feels the need to make a point, but he doesn't have time to discuss her pettiness or even to find something to eat without making himself late. He says only, "I like waffles too, you know," before kissing their daughter and leaving for work.

The house is cold and empty when he comes home that evening and the dishes are still floating in the sink. He calls his wife's cell phone, but when she answers he can barely hear her over what sounds like incredibly loud bad rock music. "Where are you?"

"At the gym," she says.

"Where's Hailey?" he asks.

"I don't know."

"You didn't pick her up from school?" He is practically shouting.

"Didn't you?" she asks, sounding out of breath. He hears a clang, like the sound of a free weight being replaced on the rack.

"But you always pick her up!"

"Yes, but you've never thanked me for doing it."

He hangs up and hops in his car. When he gets to his daughter's school, no one is waiting outside. The schoolyard gate is locked, the building's lights are all off, and all the children and their teachers are nowhere to be seen.

The joke is wearing thin now. He can't believe she could stoop so low. The more he thinks about it, the more certain he is that she hasn't. She was probably picking Hailey up when he called and was just trying to make him sweat a bit. He guesses she's pulling a prank.

He drives straight home, but his wife and daughter are still not there. A few minutes later his wife pulls into their driveway and exits her car carrying a Styrofoam cup and a takeout bag blooming with grease. Their daughter is not with her, but he's no longer worried. He's sure she's picked up Hailey and dropped her off at a friend's house as part of the prank.

"Is that dinner?" he asks.

"For me, yes." She sets down her cup and bag on the coffee table and plops down onto their couch. She's still in her gym clothes. A fine sheen of sweat glows on her forehead and at her collarbone.

"Didn't you take something down for tonight?" He is trying to be patient.

She digs around in her bag and pulls out a handful of fries. "Did you?"

"I get it," he says. "You're upset. Fine, but you didn't have to use Hailey."

His wife looks up, puzzled. "She's not here?"

"Cut it out!" he yells. "Okay, so you're mad. Teaching me a little lesson? The school for bad husbands is now in session?"

From the bag she pulls out a small carton of fries and a

cheeseburger wrapped in wax paper. She upends the bag, scattering napkins and ketchup packets all over the coffee table. "I'm just following your lead. We're only doing what we get thanked for, right? You want to be thanked every time you lift your little finger, but you don't ever thank me for all the things I do to keep this house running smoothly. In fact, you don't even see them."

"What do you mean I don't see them?" he demands. "And I do plenty around here. I help."

She unwraps her cheeseburger and eats it greedily. "Helping is when you stay in a hotel and make your own bed to save the housekeepers some time. It's when we're at a restaurant and we push our cups and plates to the end of the table to make it easier on the servers. There's no 'helping' when you're in your own home; there's only doing. You're not helping me when you braid Hailey's hair. Braiding her hair is not solely my job. Hailey is your daughter as much as she is mine. I do it every night and you've never said a word, but you do it once and we're supposed to strike the band and throw a parade?"

He stands over her, leaning down and speaking in measured tones, as if to a child. "All you have to do is tell me when you need more help. All you have to do is just tell me what needs to be done."

She points a fry at him. "I'm not the maître d' of our home. We both live here and we both have the same number of hours in each day. We both get up each morning and go to work full-time jobs in the morning, and then we both come home each evening to this same house that has to be maintained and kept up. When I see something that needs to be done, I just do it. Why do you need to be told that homes and children require continual care? Why do you have to wait for me to point this out to you?" she asks. "I signed on to be your partner, not your mother."

"Some mother," he says. "You didn't pick up Hailey!"

"Neither did you!"

"But I never pick her up."

"I know."

He pushes aside her takeout food and sits on the edge of the coffee table, facing her. He takes her hands in his and holds them between his open knees. He drops his head to his chest, closes his eyes. "All of this because of what I said last night?" he asks. His father never cooked a meal, never washed a dish, never lifted a finger. By the time he got to work this morning, the pictures he'd posted of his daughter's hair had received over a hundred likes. Men and women alike commended him—his male friends praised him for being a good father, and his women coworkers wished their husbands were as helpful as he was. He doesn't understand this tempest in a teapot over what he'd said last night. Somewhere in his wife's words about hotels, houses, and helping there's a lesson, but it's been years since he's attended school. He almost wishes he could have a do-over and go back to last night and zip shut his mouth, but even if he could somehow turn back time and do it all over, he would still want to show off, and he would still want his wife to take notice of his effort. He looks up at her now. "Is it so wrong, then, to want to be thanked?"

She rubs his knee. "Everyone wants to be appreciated."

"Please tell me where Hailey is."

"She's over at my mother's." She pushes herself up from the couch. "I'll go get her."

He waves her back into her seat. "I'll do it."

"Thank you."

"Please," he says. "Don't mention it."

Breathe

Breathe

She died earlier that day. Not a real death. With other faculty members and graduate students gathered in Vancouver for the Modern Language Association convention, she laid her body down in the convention center, closed her eyes—and died. At first she wasn't sure which position was best for the assumption of death. Should she lie facedown or repose on her back? Initially, she'd pressed her face to the floor, where the carpet abraded her cheek and scraped it near raw; she assumed that position to be the most realistic—too often had she seen black bodies cuffed and floored, cheek to ground. No, she realized, this was not the position of death, but of arrest. So she turned faceup and lay rigid as a corpse.

It felt good to die, though she did not convince herself that her actions equaled those of the youth protesters out in Ferguson, who had taken the lead and returned to protest day in and out, and who used their bodies to obstruct traffic, collapse economies, and disrupt normalcy. Nor did she liken herself to the great civil rights activists long gone and revered. She did not have to douse her eyes with milk to soothe the sting of tear gas. Nor did she have to walk through a row of hatred as racists yelled slurs and hurled bottles and eggs her way. She did not have to sit peaceably while waitresses ignored her and refused to serve her at a lunch counter. She shielded herself from no hoses, ran from no dogs, and dodged no gunfire. She died in relative safety. Dead off in Canada, a country with no experience of slavery. Dead at a conference rife with academics in a building full of registered attendants. Safe, unlike so many others. Still, when other conference attendees were filling this hour with late lunches, she was doing her part; she was at least doing something useful. She told herself that her dying counted.

As she lay dying, she wasn't sure with what to occupy her thoughts, didn't know if dying in was like a public moment of silence where you were meant to concentrate and think solely on one thing. But thinking of all the black men and women whom the police had wrongfully killed in just the past few months would ruin her silence and corrupt her death. She would surely cry if left alone with her thoughts of the slain. So instead, she mentally rehearsed bits of Hamlet's soliloquy. *To die, to sleep; to sleep, perchance to dream.* She lifted her hand to her cheek and felt the scraped skin where the carpet left its rub.

When pins and needles riddled her feet, the bodies around her rose from the ground. She followed suit, relieved to be alive once more.

Call it curiosity. She has finished her conference activities for the day—chairing her own panel, skipping lunch to squeeze in the die-in before attending the panels of her friends, making a foray through the exhibit room to peruse the new releases from her favorite academic presses—when now, intending to leave the convention center and return to her own hotel room, she sees a small crowd of conference attendees all heading toward one room and decides to tag along to see where everyone is going. She is exhausted from it all, especially the dying, but too curious not to follow.

The panel chair is offering introductions when she enters and takes a seat in the last row on the far right in the room that is quickly filling. There are thirty-five people in the audience, a good crowd for a convention like this. She'd counted only twelve at her own early morning panel. She flips through the thick pages of her conference schedule and discovers that she is at a panel on Palestine and its literature. Of the three speakers, only one name matches those listed in the program. The panel chair apologizes for the two panelists who were unable to attend. One sent only his regrets. The other has sent along his paper, to be read aloud by a designated speaker. She frowns in her back-row seat at these last-minute changes. How unprofessional to cancel at such a late date. Had they not completed their papers on time? If so, that was not a good enough reason to cancel. It was rare for anyone to arrive at the convention with a perfectly polished paper. Many participants drafted their papers on the flight over, and she'd seen too many attendees in the hotel business centers hastily banging out talking points on the hotel computers and printers for her to believe this could keep someone from making it to the convention. Perhaps there had been a funding issue. Perhaps these absent panelists had their papers accepted but had their conference funding denied. Every year, the money for conferences seemed to dwindle across the humanities. She had friends who'd had their per diems cut and some who had to pay for their own meals because their universities would now only reimburse for travel, registration, and hotel stay. Luckily, she has a new post at a well-funded university that will pay for her to attend two to three conferences per year where she can eat as much as she likes.

The first panelist's paper is on a set of translated diaries kept by a village police officer in the 1950s that he apologetically describes as boring records of visits the officer paid to his various neighbors. "That notwithstanding, these diaries are nonetheless important because of their internal dialogues and the ways in which the diaries of Palestinian villagers disrupt a western tradition of narrative that is invested in a linear and chronological method of storytelling," the panelist says.

The crowd grows during the delivery of the first paper, swelling as people filter in from other panels that have let out late or are on the other side of the convention center. Eventually, the seats are nearly all filled and several latecomers have to stand against the back wall by the entrance. It is the largest audience she has ever witnessed at an academic conference for a single panel that is not a keynote speech. How many people are here out of genuine interest and how many are accidental wanderers like her? She is the only black professor in the room. Her own area of interest is far removed from anything dealing with the Arab world or Middle Eastern culture. She is a scholar of eighteenth- and nineteenth-century African American literature and she studies the literature produced by slaves like Wheatley, Equiano, Douglass, and Jacobs; by free African American authors like Brown, Webb, Wilson, and Delaney; and later by post-Reconstruction authors like Harper, Hopkins, Chesnutt, and Dunbar. She barely dips into the early part of the twentieth century, going no further than the Harlem Renaissance, and contemporary literature she altogether eschews. What then is there to interest her in papers on the life narratives—the memoirs, biographies, diaries, and autobiographies—of Palestinian writers? What, if anything, does this have to do with her?

The next paper, the one sent in by the absent panelist, is

introduced. "This panel was conceived, proposed, and compiled several months before Israel's bombardment of Palestine this past July, but the sanctioned violence has made our panel relevant in a new way," the substitute speaker says. The speaker's voice is a whisper, her lips are too far away from the microphone, but no one lifts a hand to an ear to signal her to raise her volume. It is like two voices, two mouths, two tongues speaking at once in a murmur. The absent panelist's tongue, lying now in the speaker's mouth, is the echo of an echo.

The room is still filling. There are now more than fifty people in the audience. The year before, at the previous convention in Chicago, a panel about an academic boycott of Israel drew extraordinary attention, with journalists seeking entry in hopes of covering the proceedings. Perhaps people have come today merely to see if sparks will fly. Perhaps she should leave now, before anything gets out of hand. She has done her political duty for the day. Dying earlier has freed her from guilt. She rises to exit and inches her way behind the freestanding table at the back of the room set aside for attendees with disabilities or limited mobility, carefully navigating a wheelchair, a dog, and a cane.

Coming to the end of the paper, the substitute panelist reads the absent presenter's request for a boycott and his discussion of the recent escalation of violence in the Gaza Strip. As the absent panelist's paper is read, a clipboard containing a petition for an academic boycott of Israeli institutions makes its way across the table of the three panelists to the front left row and quickly comes down the entire left aisle before winging back up to the front right and snaking its way down to the end of the right row. "In our land we are unwanted strangers," the panelist reads. Perhaps it is because the words coming out of the panelist's mouth are the words of someone miles away that the sentence echoes in the crowded room, comes to her where she is edging along the back wall of the full room in an attempt to exit unobtrusively, roots her to the spot, and dispels the facade. Around her the bodies of black boys and men fall like shell casings. As easily as she sees the back of a woman in a Navajo-print blazer in the last row on the right, so too does she see a boy in a hood gunned down without cause; another boy detained for walking in the street, not only murdered but criminalized and defamed after death; a man placed in a chokehold, each breath bringing him closer to his last. It has been a red summer of bombs and bombardments, chokeholds, and no indictments, of die-ins and cover-ups, of violence unexcused, unjustified, and rampant. She knows nothing of the Gaza Strip, but she knows the trauma of being treated like an unwanted stranger in one's own country, knows, too, the struggle to survive in a land that has been tilled with the unpaid labor of one's ancestors and watered with the blood of one's own people.

The woman in the Navajo blanket rises from her corner seat in the last row and brings over the clipboard to her where she stands propped against the back wall. Though the room is now filled with more than sixty attendees, there are only three names on the petition. To her left, there are only two more people waiting to receive the clipboard—not enough signatures to make the petition count. Her cheek burns as if she has been slapped. She'd thought dying was all she'd have to do.

She scoots down the wall, balances the clipboard on her knees and signs her name in the waiting space. Below her signature, she forges the names of the summer's black dead. Other names come to her—too many names for one to have to know—and she writes them in as well. Lining the petition with the names of other unwanted strangers, she struggles for air, finding that she, too, cannot breathe.

Discotheque of Negroes

He works the main streets and the side ones, selling handmade necklaces. The American woman hears him before she sees him—his arm a clink and chime of cowrie shells and beads. From wrist to elbow he wears a sleeve of bracelets—ready to make a sale. Holding out his arm, he stops at her outdoor dining table and speaks in the shushing sounds of Portuguese.

"Desculpe. Não falo Portuguese," she responds, trying not to falter with her hard-learned words.

He doesn't give up easily. He repeats himself in French, then Italian. Like the menu before her, he offers her a choice of languages, but she has only her native English and four years of high school Spanish. He brightens at this. "Espagnole? Muito bem," he says, blending Italian and Portuguese as if the mix makes Spanish. He lifts his brows and smiles wolfishly, showing white teeth in dark, dark skin.

Without an invitation he takes a seat and tells her about himself. He's from Dakar, Senegal. Wolof and French are his native languages, the others he has picked up from living in Portugal. "I also have a very little English," he brags. In the mornings, he works in a fruit market. Afterward, he walks Baixa Chiado,

Rossio, and Bairro Alto, selling African jewelry to tourists. He shares an apartment with three other Africans, all of whom can be seen similarly peddling jewelry on the main streets and in the squares.

He angles his chair closer to hers, pulling it near so that it scrapes on the small slippery cobblestones. The bracelets slide up and down his arms as he places his elbows on the table and leans in, wanting to know all about her. How long will she stay in Lisbon? Who accompanies her? Husband and children? Is this her first trip to Portugal? Is America very hot, very big?

The waitress circles the table, ready to shoo away the peddler, looking to the American woman for a signal, but she ignores her. He is no bother, not a menace. What harm is there in him? Though he had initially approached her with vending in mind, it is obvious that he stays out of male interest. Dressed in a white cotton shirt rolled back at the elbows, clad in blue jeans, and shod in soccer shoes, he is tall, thin, and utterly black, with skin as dark as only that of one whose people had never crossed the middle passage could ever be. In him she finds nothing to fear. What she fears in Lisbon are pickpockets who will steal her money and her passport, leaving her forever stranded in Europe. To avoid this, she wears her bag slung across her body, tucking only forty euros in its zippered sleeve, leaving the rest hidden back in her hotel room two blocks away on Rua da Assunção, where a polyglot concierge holds her key at the front desk and keeps her passport in a safety deposit box. She has a care for her safety, but she also trusts her instincts, which tell her there is no danger from this man who sits across from her, scanning his repertoire of languages to find one for her, making portmanteaus out of words, speaking a hodgepodge—*Sportuguenglish*—just to keep her talking.

Her eyes linger on a bangle at his wrist, a smoky swirl of cream and cloud. He takes it off and slides it onto her right arm. "Sorte," he says. For luck.

The waitress cleans off the table behind them. Grown bolder, she approaches their table, reaching for the American woman's plate. "May I?"

She stalls the waitress. She hasn't finished the salad that comes with every dish she orders, though the dressing is only ever oil and vinegar. The waitress steps back and tilts her head in the man's direction. "Tudo bem?"

"Sim," the American woman answers, nodding. "Tudo bem."

He answers too, moving first through English, then Spanish, then Portuguese. "Yes. We are friends now. Amigos. Tudo bem."

Here in Lisbon everything is tudo bem this and tudo bem that and everywhere one goes it is tudo bem, tudo bem, tudo bem. As long as she is here, this is true. All is well. Everything is fine and anything is better than the world back at home, where black churches were being burned like kindling, and black people were being tackled, slammed, asphyxiated, arrested, and killed for selling loose cigarettes, for failing to signal a lane change when driving, for praying, for swimming, for walking, for breathing.

She asks him where all the black people are.

"Two of us, we are right here," he says, again showing the teeth that make his skin seem darker.

She presses on. Where do the black people go for fun? Are there good places to dance?

Yes, and he knows them all. There is a place for each night. They can go out tonight to find one.

What kind of music should she expect?

African music. Souk. Perhaps some reggae.

What about hip-hop?

"You Americans love the hip-hop," he says. "Sorry, minha senhora, but only a little will be at the discotheque of Negroes."

She can't help but laugh at his phrasing. It's the fault of the language they've chosen to meet in, the Portuguese he tries to pass off as Spanish simply by changing his accent. In her pocket-sized phrasebook the official word for nightclub is *discoteca*, a word so formal, so old-fashioned, that it conjures bygone days for her, calling to mind an old episode of *The Jeffersons*—the one where George, Weezy, Tom, and Helen all left their Upper East Side luxury apartment for a night of disco dancing. His words give her a glittering ball dangling from the ceiling; men in wide-lapelled jackets; women in tube tops and hot pants; roller skates on everyone; jive turkeys and hot mamas all getting down and doing the Batman, the bump, the funky chicken, the hustle, and the penguin as they come down the Soul Train Line.

"Please. What is it funny?" His smile is wide and waiting.

"American humor," she says. "Desculpe."

She is laughing neither at him nor with him, but how to say it? She has no language to let him in on the joke, no words to say how wistful he has made her—how she longs for his discotheque of Negroes—how laughter is her only shield from the ache of knowing that as soon as she leaves this place, it will all come back to her, that she will fly home to a summer of senseless slaughter, of black lives that don't matter.

She signals for the check. Unzipping the sleeve of her bag, she pulls out her money envelope and removes a ten-euro bill, knowing she'll be leaving a larger than customary tip. Rising to leave, she writes down her hotel's address on a napkin so he can find her later. Tonight, they'll look but fail to find it, this discotheque of

Negroes, this place that is not a real place, that is neither here nor there, that is merely a misunderstanding, a place born of tangled tongues and smatterings of language they've conjured between them and cobbled into meaning, a place that is long gone lost.

"Tudo bem?" he asks, clutching her scribbled-on napkin.

"Tudo bem," she answers.

But of course it is a lie. Everything is not fine. Nothing will ever be fine again.

Elevator

She can't let the elevator break her down. *Oh no, let's go,* she thinks when the white boys get on after her. She wants to make a run for it, but the doors close too quickly. She shrinks into a corner, hoping to go unseen, praying the white boys keep facing forward.

"Some fun," one says.

"Gotta do that again," says the other. His blond hair wisps out beneath his MAKE AMERICA GREAT AGAIN ball cap and he tucks in the strands before pressing the button for their floor—her floor. Her stomach drops as the elevator ascends. She's not afraid of heights, but white boys are another thing. They're terrorists—blithely they bomb schools and burn black churches, and afterward they go for burgers with the cops; they enter elementary schools with automatic weapons and gun down innocent children and their teachers, then walk away from their mayhem, slapped with fines and orders for counseling. They flaunt tiki torches and ram their cars into innocent women; they rape unconscious girls behind dumpsters on college campuses and then beg not to let their crimes interfere with their swimming careers. They destroy everything they touch.

A quiver starts in her soles and fear trembles all through her body. She shouldn't have to feel this way; the feeling is a terror on her skin. When she checked in last night at this extended-stay hotel, how was she to know she would awaken to a bevy of white boys? Plain dumb luck has it that her stay coincides with a daylong meeting of law enforcement officers. This morning, at breakfast, she saw a group of uniformed white boys coming out of the meeting room, saw others on the computers in the business center, while still more white boys emerged from the dining area, stirring their coffees, plates piled with mini donuts. Initially, she mistook them for airline pilots until she saw the way they looked at her—their eyes flicking over her and then up toward the security cameras—no mistaking those looks that said they wanted to take her down for the crime of her skin. If it weren't for the cameras and the watchful front desk clerks, she'd have checked out immediately. Her criminality is inescapable. She has breathed, swum in the pool, had coffee—she's even wearing a hoodie—all offenses for which black people have been arrested and killed. Who can say that riding an elevator while black is not now the newest crime? She wonders if this will be her last elevator ride.

Had she seen these two earlier? White boys—so hard to tell them apart. They could be officers too, only dressed in plain clothes now that their sessions are over—the possibility only makes her more afraid. She's seen the footage, knows what white cops do. Just the other day, in Philadelphia, white cops arrested two black men for sitting in a Starbucks to wait for a friend. The two men had been in the coffee shop for only two minutes when a barista—a young white girl—called the cops on them for trespassing. The two men were terrorized, harassed, and cuffed, all to soothe white fear. Down in Alabama, a white clerk at the Waffle House called the cops on a black woman who asked for plastic cutlery. Two burly white police officers tackled the innocent woman to the ground, wrestling her so hard they exposed her breasts, all the while threatening to break her arms.

The elevator makes no stops. For the next five floors it's just the three of them.

The one with the hat looks over his shoulder and catches sight of her. "What floor?" he asks.

The other one turns. He gestures at the double row of buttons beside the framed certificate of operation. Just below the sign for the hotel's free hot breakfast, the button for their floor—her floor—glows. "What—floor—you—want?" he asks, speaking slowly, carefully, as if she doesn't speak English.

The mirrorlike chrome walls of the elevator's interior double the white boys, quadrupling her fear. She shakes her head as if uncomprehending, allowing them—encouraging them—to recast her as any ethnicity that will keep her safe.

The white boy in the hat reaches into his pocket for something and she clutches her purse, holding it in front of her so they can see it for what it is. She knows how magical black hands are. They can turn anything—lipstick, cell phone, keys, Skittles—into a gun right before white eyes.

Will they follow her when she gets off?

She calls to mind the layout on her floor, searching her memory for security cameras. There's the tall entryway table opposite the elevator doors. On it sits a phone just like the one in her room—the sign above it says to dial 1 for front desk. On either side of the table are receptacles for waste and recycling. And above, in the corners of the ceilings? No security cameras, just a sign on the sliver of wall between the two elevators: IN FIRE EMERGENCY DO NOT USE ELEVATORS USE EXIT STAIRS.

She presses the button for the very next floor. When the doors open, she exits without appearing to hurry, careful to make no sudden moves, but once out of the elevator, she takes off in a run. Dashing for the stairwell, she crashes right into a cleaning cart and almost knocks it over. Two housekeepers help her up, fussing and clucking over her in affectionate, solicitous Spanish. Who knows what they are saying? It's their brown faces that arrest her, making it so she can breathe again. It's simply the harmless way they look at her, as if she is merely a person and not a crime, that eases her fear and slows her beating heart.

Tears on Tap

The password is *Becky*. As soon as she whispers it, the bouncer urges her forward, clips the velvet rope behind her, and lets her into the hottest, newest bar in town. She edges her way through the thick throng of all the beautiful black people who have found this secret place just as she has, who—like herself—have been seeking it for so long. She angles her body sidewise to squeeze between the barely walkable spaces among the groups of friends and colleagues, the couples or couples-in-the-making, the old heads looking for women to impress, the women who do not impress easily. The premium spirits are lined in rows and tiers behind the bar, illuminated by soft lighting, their labels easy and clear to read. She's not here for them. Like everyone else in the crowded bar tonight, she's here to taste the new drink on tap.

She hovers nears the bar, waiting for a seat. A young man settles his tab and she slides onto his vacated stool. The bartender retrieves the tip and takes her order. "What can I get you?"

"The new new," she says.

This new bar, it was said, had white girl tears on tap. Lately, there was such an excess of them, such a plethora, that the owner had come up with the idea to harvest them like hops and grapes.

The rest of the process (fermentation? distillation?) he kept secret. Rumor had it that he'd culled tears from the woman who'd called the police on the black family having a cookout at a park in Oakland, from the barista who'd called the cops on two black men drinking coffee at a Starbucks in Philly, from the cashier who'd called the cops on the patron at the Waffle House who'd simply asked for cutlery, from the off-duty policewoman who entered a young black man's apartment and shot him dead and then claimed she'd mistaken his apartment for hers and thought *he* was the intruder, and even from the missionary who pretended to be a doctor and caused the deaths of hundreds of children in Uganda with her fake medical diagnoses and treatments, but no one knew for sure. The owner was cagey about who, where, and when. Certainly there was no shortage of white girl tears—every time a Becky got caught and called out for taking it upon herself to monitor and police a black body, she cried buckets—really, the owner could have gotten those tears from anywhere.

The bartender holds a glass at a forty-five-degree angle one inch below the tap faucet and grips the tap handle near the base, pulling it forward to open the flow. Once the glass is half full, he slowly tilts it upright to complete his pour. He places before her a pale pink drink with a one-inch head of foam.

On either side of her the other patrons are drinking the same. "Must be good," she predicts.

"Everyone tastes something different," the bartender says, wiping down the counter.

"Bottoms up."

The drink is tart and tangy, bitter and sweet. It puckers her lips and curls her tongue. This is a drink to put hair on one's chest.

She's caught by the drink's complexity, by the way it pours

like beer yet tastes like wine. She expects the white girl tears to taste like pumpkin spice, like lattes and Pilates, like yoga pants and asparagus, like fringed scarves and sheepskin boots, like flat asses and lack of rhythm, like tanning beds, like lip and butt injections—which it does—but in the body of the drink the subtle notes of other flavors emerge, and once she drinks past the foam she tastes bouquets of bias, caches of past cruelties. With each sip she tastes the pain of memories. Like the time her freshman roommate offered to fix her up on a blind date because she was *so pretty for a black girl*. Like the time her elementary school principal asked her to let someone else—someone white—win for a change. Halfway through the drink, the white girl tears taste like the time her colleagues invited her at the last minute to join their panel proposal because a diversity element would improve their chances of acceptance; like all the times she went out shopping for clothes or food and white women stopped her to ask about merchandise or produce or sales or aisles because they assumed she worked there.

The bartender looks over, eyebrow raised, to see if she wants another, but one is more than enough. Determined to finish, she drinks down to the dregs; where the flavor is at its strongest; where the tears taste like a moment she'll never forget—that time her teacher, a white woman, lopped off one of her braids in front of the class and then told her to stop crying because *it was just hair and it would grow back*, uncaring that it was never *just hair* to a black girl fated to spend the rest of her life being told to change her hair (press and curl it, blow it out, wrap it up) if she ever wanted to get a job and keep it, if she ever wanted to earn a living, if she ever wanted to be beautiful, if she ever wanted to be enough; where those last few drops, tasting of that time she first learned to swallow pain, leave an aftertaste, a bitter residue on her tongue, of when the self of a girl was first severed in two.

Mean to Me

This is the part where the white girl cries. You tell her no she can't touch your hair and try to explain why, but she's not listening because she's collapsed into tears. Right before your eyes her bangs flatten, her chin droops, and her thin lips quiver. Why are you being so mean to me, she whines; but you can't answer, because her question brings up memories of albums with Lady Day's face on the cover, white gardenias framing her from temple to cheek, and you hear Billie Holiday's bruised, brave, addicted, and addicting voice drawling that famous song; but you can't answer because that song reminds you of the fight with your college boyfriend over whether Lady Day or Sarah Vaughan sang it better, and he thought the answer was obvious—Vaughan's voice was so much smoother and more controlled, after all, and he was enrolled in a history of jazz course so he should know—but you didn't give up so easily because Billie Holiday had been your bread and butter as a child when every other kid was eating Froot Loops or Cream of Wheat, which is to say that your mother fed it to you—literally—whenever she wanted to keep you quiet, which is to say that when she pulled the record from its cardboard sleeve and touched the needle to it and Billie Holiday's voice leapt from the vinyl to you where you sat beside the hi-fi, you brought the record's sleeve to your mouth and clenched it between your teeth so you could hear the song better, and later, when someone told you in grad school that Thomas Edison chomped the wood of his phonograph to better hear the music, you understood completely even though you are not now and have never been deaf, yes, your mother fed you Lady Day's music and you consumed it all, just as you read the autobiography *Lady Sings the Blues* and watched the movie with Diana Ross, so you know all there is to know about Lady Day, who clearly sang the song better than Sarah Vaughan despite her voice's lack, and you know this despite your decision not to take the history of jazz class with him, which is really what the argument was about beneath all the posturing and the chatter; but you can't answer because you listened again to Sarah Vaughan's version years later when there was no college boyfriend to argue her case, and her voice argued it all by itself so that you weren't sure anymore and declared it a tie; but you can't answer because for a second you almost think of the Doris Day version and have to force yourself to think about something else; otherwise this would be a completely different story.

Karen

Her sister was late with the Juneteenth piñata. The family had already begun to arrive. Relatives filed out of their cars and came straight into the backyard, eager for the festivities.

Ignoring the grill, the picnic table, the lawn and deck chairs, the coolers teeming with ice, chilled beers, wine coolers, and sodas, the small square tables with fresh decks of cards just waiting to be shuffled and cut, her relatives crossed the yard's wide expanse of low-cut grass and came to stand directly in front of the large oak tree from which no piñata hung. "Where is it?" they asked, all frowning.

"It's coming," she told them. "It's on the way." She made her way to each of her aunts and uncles and each of their spouses and each of her cousins, pacifying them individually.

"I hope we didn't come here for nothing," her aunt by marriage said. "We drove a long way."

"Your mother wouldn't like you playing us for fools," her uncle said.

"I promise it's on the way." She put her uncle in charge of the grill, hoping to distract him.

He took up the meat tongs and clicked them at her in accusation. "You know she took this tradition very seriously."

Yes, she knew. It was here in the backyard of this house, which she and her sister had inherited from their parents, that the tradition had begun. Lamenting that the only time the family ever saw one another was at funerals, their mother had begun inviting family from near and far over for a Juneteenth celebration. Their mother had made the piñata herself that first year; she'd spent weeks sewing and stuffing it. Once finished, their father had proudly hung it high from the oak tree in their backyard. Years later now, their parents were gone and she and her sister used store-bought piñatas; other than that, they stuck to the tradition and kept the ritual alive.

For half an hour she tended to her relatives, setting up games of spades and bid whist at the card tables, putting her college-bound cousin in charge of the music, monitoring her younger cousins who ran in and out of the house, swinging the screen door hard enough to unhinge it. Finally, her sister appeared at the gate holding an unwieldy package in both arms, carrying it like a child.

She ran over to help and unlatched the gate. "What took you so long? Everyone's already here."

Her sister was out of breath. "You should have seen it. I had to fight tooth and nail. This was the last one."

She ripped open the plastic bag and peered inside. "I asked for Becky."

"I wrestled a deaconess for this! She almost knocked me down." Her sister wiped sweat from her brow. Her shirt was wet with perspiration. "You couldn't have done any better."

"Put it over by the oak," she said, refusing to take the bait. "Uncle Roy will do the honors."

Summoned, their uncle left the grill and came over. He tore the rest of the bag away and held up the promised piñata, a three-foot-long papier-mâché white woman. The white woman's short blond hair was cut into an asymmetrical spiky style. Her face was done in the garish makeup of the 1990s—cat-eye eyeliner, glittery eye shadow, and frosty lip gloss. She wore a painted-on outfit: V-neck top with three-quarter-length sleeves, khaki capri pants, and a pair of Crocs.

He gave the limp effigy the once-over, recognizing the woman by her thin lips and perpetual scowl. Karen. Yes, this was the woman who skipped to the front of the line and demanded to see a manager and refused to wait her turn. This was the woman who viewed him with suspicion as he went about his day, minding his business. This was the woman who could make a phone call that would get him killed. "Looks just like her," he said, gripping the papier-mâché woman by the neck as he dragged her to the tree.

The Karen piñata claimed everyone's attention. They laid their cards facedown and left their games; they covered their plates with napkins and left their food; they forgot the meat on the grill and let it burn; they looped the music and let it play.

Patiently, they stood by and watched carefully as Uncle Roy tied a rope around the white woman's neck and secured the string around a sturdy branch to hoist her high. They'd waited all year for this.

As a girl she hadn't understood all the fuss. That first year she'd chided her parents, "Don't you feel bad about doing this?"

She never forgot her mother's look of scorn. "She called the cops on us—a noise complaint. We were in the old apartment and your sister was teething and crying all hours of the night." Her mother had then slipped the blindfold over her eyes. She'd yelled, "She called the cops on a baby!" and had swung at the piñata with all of her might.

"The cops use our pictures as target practice at the gun range," her father had said as he'd reached for the club and donned the blindfold for his turn.

With adulthood, she'd found her own reasons and had come to know what drove her relatives to gather for this destructive act. Maturity taught her why, there in the backyard surrounded by a high wooden fence, they felt the need to do in the shade what was done to them in the glare of the sun.

Her relatives formed an unruly line, jockeying for position at the base of the tree.

"Let me at it," her college-bound cousin said, jostling to the front.

"Age before beauty," an aunt said, pulling his collar.

"I'm a crack shot," Uncle Roy bragged, stepping forward.

Impatient and eager, they all clamored for the club and begged for the blindfold. She could hardly blame them. Everyone had their reasons. Everyone wanted to be first.

Monument

It was her turn to take the baby. Her husband didn't even ask where she was going. He knew where she always took the baby. To the square. Always to the square. There was something there the baby needed to see.

She made sure to park the stroller as close as possible to the famous monument. She made sure to pack a lunch—she didn't want to end up running back home for something as trifling as hunger.

Some days she could get as close to the statue as she dared. Today was such a day. When she sat this near, she didn't need her sunglasses or her bucket hat, and she could push back the canopy of the stroller without the baby catching too much sun. The tall bronze statue of Nat Turner cast a protective shadow and provided precious shade, allowing her and the baby to find respite and bask in their history all at once. Only a few other families were out this afternoon. Luckily, there were no protesters come to flank the monument and ruin her outing. The protesters said the statue's presence was offensive to the families and the descendants of all the white slave owners Nat Turner and his group had killed on the night of his 1831 rebellion. For years, protesters had been agitating for the statue's removal, an action she could neither understand nor condone.

This statue would never come down if she had anything to say about it. Protesters called it an eyesore—to her it was anything but. How she enjoyed looking up at Nat Turner's strong face and into his fierce eyes. She couldn't imagine anyone taking Nat away, couldn't envision coming to the square and not seeing him. Though Turner's rebellion had been a lost cause, his goal had been admirable—freedom from the tyranny of slavery. Some called him a murderer, but she believed he was a true patriot. She would always tell their baby the truth about him. She and her husband would bring their child here, year after year, to grow in the shadow of the proud statue.

She lifted the baby's arm and waved its hand at the monument. "Do you want to say hi to Nat? Say hi to Mr. Turner."

The baby cooed and gurgled. They played this little game every time they came. She shook the baby bottle and watched the baby's bright eyes gleam. "Do you think Nat is hungry? Do you want me to give him some of your ba-ba?" she asked. "Or should I give him some of my trail mix? Even heroes get hungry, you know."

"What a thing to say!"

The voice she heard seemed to come from nowhere. On the other side of the statue stood a frumpy middle-aged white woman with short, cropped blond hair. She asked the white woman, "Are you talking to me?"

"A hero? Really?"

Most of the white people gave her a wide berth when she was by the statue, subjecting her to hostile glares, yet never approaching. Today, the white woman came closer and said, "I don't see how you can sit here at ease in front of such a terrible monument."

"It's my history and my child's history," she answered. "I'm here to remind myself of it."

"You know, a lot of people died that night," the white woman said. She jabbed her finger at Nat Turner. "And he killed them! Slaughtered them in their beds!"

"Slave owners," she corrected the woman, unable to keep the shrug from her voice. "And he led a group of innocent victims to the freedom which was rightly theirs." She soothed her baby, who had begun to fuss, and tucked the thin summer blanket tightly around the tiny limbs. "The price of freedom is high, and those who would deny others from having it might have to lose their lives."

Tears gathered in the white woman's eyes, her chin trembled, and her face went splotchy. "Don't you care how much pain this statue causes? It's a monument that celebrates the slaughter of my ancestors. My great-great-grandparents could have been among the people *he* killed, and I have to see this hurtful thing every time I come out here. It isn't right."

She could not relate to the woman's personal ordeal. After all, the statue's presence did not pain *her*, so how could it be painful? The monument was an important part of her heritage, a reminder that long before any Emancipation Proclamation, her people had fought to claim their freedom, even on pain of death. That was worth commemorating. That was worth remembering for all time.

She patted her baby once more for good measure and then stood to meet the white woman. She warned, "If you're thinking of harming Nat, you'll have to go through me."

"Are you threatening me?" the white woman asked.

"Yes."

The white woman sputtered and plunked her hands on her

hips. "Imagine if this was a statue of a slaveholder instead! Robert E. Lee or Jefferson Davis. Imagine if every time you came here, you had to come face-to-face with someone who stood for enslaving your people. Imagine the pain you would feel. How would you like this statue then?"

Imagine that! Statues erected of the Confederates, who had threatened to sever the union in two, committed treason against the country, and then lost the war to boot? Monuments of losers? Commemorating traitors—what a ridiculous notion. What an absurd rewriting of history. To the victor went the spoils—everyone knew that.

She laughed in the white woman's face at such a foolish idea. She laughed so hard that the white woman backed away in fear. She laughed so hard that the baby caught her laughter and joined in, laughing along with her. She laughed so hard she feared she might never stop—it was just that funny. Who could imagine such foolishness? It was the most preposterous thing she'd ever heard.

Dismissal

She waits for me by the curb outside the public elementary school while other kids gather to walk home together. A lucky few get whisked away, ushered into cars far better than mine. It is after three; dismissal's come and gone. I'm running late but on my way, almost there. This she does not know.

Other parents have real cars, not clunkers that drive on a whim. They have better work hours, better schedules, better everything. I'm doing the best I can. Sometimes ends never meet.

If I had it my way, she'd be in a different school. A private one. Or maybe just a better one, where the schoolyard is a place for kids to play, not for teachers to park their cars. A school where they don't need metal detectors to deter fifth and sixth graders from coming in with weapons. A school where the scaffolding eventually comes down because the repairs actually get completed. A school where they let kids wait inside instead of hurrying them outdoors to leave them unsupervised in the cold.

Stuck three cars behind the light, I see her, a tiny thing tucked into the shadow of the building's scaffold. Her body tells the story of waiting—the fingers plucking the straps of her backpack, the head hanging low, the small frame hunching beneath the toll of all those minutes in which I have failed to show. She doesn't have a watch, so she can't count the minutes; instead she counts the ways in which I disappoint her. Or maybe she thinks of all the reasons I might not make it, wonders if I'm dead somewhere, slumped over the steering wheel of my car, shot by the officer who stopped me on my way to her. She already knows that this is a thing that can happen to people who look like us. Or maybe she's reciting our address and phone number and wondering who she might go to in order to tell them she's lost. The teachers are all gone for the day, and she knows to never, ever call the police. Finally, I pull up to the curb and honk and she looks up, surprised and relieved. I wait for her to say how she was scared that I wasn't coming, but when she climbs into the car, she asks me only what took so long.

Reminder

For two weeks she's in Lisbon attending a conference on Fernando Pessoa, a poet she's never heard of although there are statues of him all over the city. Every day, tourists gather at the bronze statue of him sitting in front of a café, but the one she likes best is the one where he stands tall and has a book on his shoulders instead of a head. The conference is a perfect distraction from all the turmoil at home; being a busy tourist makes a certain type of forgetting easy. She's booked a room in a watchful hotel, one where it's impossible to enter or exit without passing the concierge, one where every guest must be announced, and the concierge holds your key while you're out, one the other conference attendees avoid so they can have indiscriminate sex with strangers free of surveillance. Each morning she comes down for what the hotel advertises as a continental breakfast but is just an offering of two crusty hard rolls, four pats of butter, jam, and a pot of the strongest coffee she's ever had—it takes the entire small pitcher of cream just to make the heart-attack-inducing stuff drinkable. After breakfast each day she leaves for a morning of workshops, an afternoon of panels and presentations, and an evening of drinking ginjinha from shot glasses made of chocolate as she joins the other conference goers at the miradouros and looks out over the city.

Today she's left the conference and its attendees behind on the Chiado side of the city, opting to spend her afternoon on the Baixa side, where it's sunnier and less congested. The beauty of Lisbon is painful to behold. Everything she sees hurts: the water so blue, the seafood so fresh, the ginjinha so sweet, the coffee so strong. She needs the afternoon off. So here she is, descending fourteen shallow steps, making her way down the flat plateau that takes her to the water's edge and the mouth of the Rio Tejo. Here she sits on a stone stairway sleek with water spray in the westernmost corner of the world. Pigeons wander on the steps, their coral feet sure on the sunbaked stones, their small heads leading the way, their slick black compact bodies following. To her left, a sightseeing cruise ship pulls out from the harbor and two men in red EDP shirts demolish a sand crocodile sculpture, bringing buckets of seawater to wash away their first try so they can start over with newly dampened sand. Here by the water-front, where it is not exactly clean, with Lisboans beside and be-hind her, she sits on the shallow wave-washed steps, among the cigarette butts and small pieces of trash left by others, while the tourists walk to the edge and obscure the view to take selfies and clap at birds. Here she looks out onto the water, out past the two tall columns, out past a Golden Gate–like bridge and a statue of Christ with arms outstretched, and out into the harbor to see the boats and their sails and the crashing green waves, imagining the unimaginable world beyond the sea. Seated at the water's edge it's easy to understand how people could have long ago presumed the earth to be flat, for who could look at this vast expanse of water and believe there could be life on the other side of it?

At the mouth of the Rio Tejo an old hippie with long curling gray hair feeds the seagulls even though it is forbidden. Standing close to the water, his book bag hanging from his shoulder, his faded cargo pants wet at the cuffs, his shirt green as the sea, he pulls fat chunks of lanche bread from a plastic sack and whistles for the gulls' attention. Pinching bread between his fingers, he raises his arm high and a seagull swoops down to snatch the morsel clean from his hand. He ignores the gulls that flock to him and peck around his feet, holding the bread high, making the birds fly up to meet him. If they want to eat, first they must soar. Twenty pigeons flock near the man's feet, surrounding him like something out of a Hitchcock movie. She's never seen so many birds so up close before—she can see the red of a pigeon's eye. She scoots back against the smooth flat steps, giving way to the man standing in the midst of so many birds, so calm and happy with his colony of seagulls and loft of pigeons, so unafraid of what he has summoned. He reminds her of herself, of a story her mother once told her from back when she was a baby and her whole family still lived in Bed-Stuy on a block she cannot recall. Her mother said, "I'll never get over that time we took you to Prospect Park and the birds came for you. You were still in your stroller and you loved showing off, climbing out of your stroller while it was still moving just to show that you could. I'd saved my hot dog bun so you could feed the birds. Well, you took that bun and shimmied out of your stroller and went right over to this group of pigeons before I could catch you. The next thing I know all these birds came out of nowhere and went straight to you. I'd never been so scared in my life! The birds were all around you, and you weren't much bigger than they were. I couldn't get to you, they had you surrounded. All I saw were wings. I was shouting and shooing them away, and when they flew off, there you were, a little bitty thing just smiling and laughing."

She's sorry now, forty years later, for the terror she caused her mother so long ago.

Though it's been easy to lose herself in the conference-sponsored literary tourism, to attend the workshops and panels by day and to sit by the miradouros at night, today when she leaves from the crowd of attendees to go her own way there's less escaping than she expects and the city becomes a reminder. The small slick cobblestones that line the city streets remind her of grad school days in Philadelphia and of nights spent dancing in Olde City and of leaving the nightclub and walking for several blocks before getting a taxi to stop for her and of bruising her feet on those hard cobblestones meant only for carriages and horses and Betsy Ross and Benjamin Franklin; the steep hills of Lisbon take her back to her undergraduate days in the Bay Area and to taking the Caltrain north to San Francisco for dorm-sponsored treasure hunts and roaming Haight-Ashbury until her shins burned and glowed; but the metro station she crosses through to get from Baixa to Chiado and back again takes her all the way back to childhood, all the way back to Brooklyn.

When she walks through the Baixa-Chiado station, those blue-and-white-tiled walls remind her of that scene in *The Wiz* where Michael Jackson, Diana Ross, Nipsey Russell, the lion, and Dorothy's dog Toto all eased on down the road and followed its yellow bricks down into a blue-and-white-tiled subway station where they were menaced by a peddler and the scariest balloon puppets ever, a scene she had nightmares about as a kid and still won't watch as an adult, although there are different dangers now—instead of peddlers, puppets, and garbage cans with fangs out to kill, there are bigots coming out of hiding, shucking off their hoods, and using their badges to snuff black lives so that she has to leave the country for weeks at a time just to take a deep breath, because every inhalation is an act of rebellion, because every breath she now draws is a transgression. Remembering that parts of *The Wiz*, a movie made a year after her birth, were filmed down in the Hoyt-Schermerhorn Streets Station on the A line in downtown Brooklyn reminds her that Hoyt-Schermerhorn is the stop where she and her family always got off when they went to the movies, which reminds her that when the Loew's Metropolitan closed, she'd been just a teenager, which had been the end of having nice things, because that had been the only movie theater left in downtown Brooklyn, because the Duffield had been shuttered a few years earlier, back when she was thirteen, because someone had shot up the movie theater during the airing of *New Jack City*, which is to say that—truly—there is no place like home.

Caretaking

Housegirl

ousegirl was what Mrs. McAllister had recently begun to call her personal home-care attendant. She'd heard the term in a movie somewhere, no doubt, some movie featuring a buxom star from the forties—a blond if the black-and-white footage could be believed—languishing on a lounge chair while the housegirl carried in smelling salts on a silver lacquered tray. She had definitely not read the term in a book. Mrs. McAllister was not given over to much reading lately. The flipping of the pages, the propping of the spine, and the adjusting of the eyes to the tiny indecipherable print was too much of a bother since the stroke. Now she had no feeling in her left arm; it hung lifeless by her side, an uninvited guest too rude to leave.

TV was easier, especially since one of her nieces had bought her a VCR last Christmas. Now Mrs. McAllister could watch videos all day. She was always getting tapes in the mail from relatives who felt guilty about not visiting. She had quite the collection now. A boxed set of *Bonanza*. The Duke's old movies. *Mahogany*. *Sounder*. *Claudine*. Two copies of every movie Sean Connery had ever made, just in case. And a bunch of blaxploitation movies her nephew had sent as a joke. Just recently Mrs. McAllister had received *Ghost* and *Dirty Dancing* and been introduced to Patrick

Swayze, whom she could watch over and over without getting bored. Every time she watched him twist and turn, she thought to herself: *Nice butt for a white boy.*

She didn't have much to do besides watch her tapes. No one ever came to visit her anymore. Her relatives complained that she ignored them, leaving them in the living room while she shouted out to them through her opened bedroom door. They didn't understand how difficult getting out of bed truly was. She couldn't do it on her own. The housegirl had to come and help her; she had to roll her to one side before Mrs. McAllister could prop herself up with her good arm and get her right leg to moving. She didn't want her family to see her like that; she didn't want to be a bother. Early on into her recovery, Mrs. McAllister had learned to anticipate her own needs. She could predict a trip to the bathroom ten minutes before she actually felt the pressing need in her bladder. Ten minutes it took her to drag her dead leg down the hallway and make it to the bathroom, where her special toilet seat awaited her. Now she no longer had to squat. Her nurse had ordered her a raised plastic toilet seat and had rails installed on the sides of the toilet in case Mrs. McAllister should fall again. To make things easier. "Too late for that," Mrs. McAllister had told her.

"Better late than never" had been the nurse's reply.

Now, the bathroom reminded her of a hospital's. No doubt, her relatives didn't like that when they came to visit either. No doubt that kept them away as well.

She didn't mind that they didn't visit. The TV and VCR kept her from loneliness. Besides, she had her housegirl, and the girl did a fine job keeping house.

Mrs. McAllister really had no idea what kind of job the housegirl did. She hadn't seen her own living room in over a year.

The walk was too difficult. Besides, there was nothing she needed from that room anyway. The TV had already been moved to her bedroom. The living room was now just a shell, full of furniture, waiting for guests that never showed.

During her shift, the housegirl sat in the living room, close enough if needed, yet out of the way so as not to intrude. Out in the living room she never made a sound.

Mrs. McAllister supposed that the housegirl, a quiet woman with thick black hair and an even thicker accent, read in the living room until her shift was done. But really, she didn't know. She didn't know much about the housegirl at all. Not even her name. Or her age. Over eighteen, she supposed, but you could never tell these days. The housegirl kept her nappy hair in two braids that followed the shape of her head, and she wore silent rubber shoes. Sometimes Mrs. McAllister would turn down the sound on her television and listen for the housegirl. She would hear her when she was cooking in the kitchen, and then only the distinct sounds of water running in the sink, the refrigerator door opening, but never the sound of the housegirl's shoes.

The housegirl was supposed to bathe her every day, to help her sit on her shower stool and wash the hard-to-reach parts. But she bathed her only once a week and Mrs. McAllister let her get away with it. There was no one to lie beside her, and she had grown used to the smell of her own skin.

The housegirl didn't have to feed her; she could still do that herself. Sometimes, though, she needed help opening jars and bottles. She couldn't hold a can opener, couldn't twist open a bottle of soda or open a jar of pickles. She couldn't have pickles anyway; the doctors didn't want her having salty things that would shoot her blood pressure up. But every once in a while she was able to convince the housegirl to bring her a bag of potato chips. Salt and vinegar. Onion and garlic. Sour cream and onion. Mrs. McAllister didn't care what kind. The saltier the better. After eating them, she would have the housegirl split the small bag open. Then Mrs. McAllister would lick her finger and run it over the plastic insides of the bag, collecting whatever leftover crumbs and remnants of flavor she could find, trying to make it last.

She tried to make the housegirl like her by being an easy patient, but every day the housegirl was still eager to leave. Most days Mrs. McAllister didn't want her to. *Stay*, she would think.

Stalling for time, Mrs. McAllister would ask, "Did you wash and dry the dishes? Is everything tidied up?"

Pretending not to understand her, the housegirl would pat her hands and talk to her like a child.

"Everything is all tidied up," she'd say.

"You didn't forget anything?"

"All done now. Bye-bye."

Mrs. McAllister would want to pull her back and say: *Don't leave.*

Instead she would let the housegirl go. "Don't be late tomorrow," she'd call behind the housegirl, turning the volume up on her television to drown out the sound of her front door closing.

Caretaking

Winsome gets off the 3 train at Saratoga and Livonia, already late. Walking quickly past the dilapidated public park already filled with crackheads at this early hour, she ignores truant teenagers playing handball and heads for the nearest bodega. Standing in front of the wire rack of snacks, she eyes askance the rows of cheese curls, corn chips, and pretzels. Despite the recent warnings of Mrs. McAllister's niece, Winsome contemplates the prohibited snacks. Bristling now, thinking of the niece, Winsome grabs four bags embossed with owls and throws a dollar onto the counter to procure the forbidden bounty.

Last week that niece had arrived unannounced, on a rare visit, just after Winsome had opened a bag for Mrs. McAllister. The young woman had walked into the apartment looking like so many of the women Winsome saw getting off the subway in Manhattan, dressed in business suits with socks and sneakers, heading for offices where they traded their Nikes for dark pumps. Women with degrees, not certificates. Winsome sensed the hurry in her, catching it in the way she'd stared above Mrs. McAllister's head at the clock on the wall and glanced a kiss across her aunt's cheek, lips barely touching skin. The niece saw the chips and snatched the bag away, slapping her aunt's hand as if she were a naughty child.

"Winsome, please don't give her any more of this junk, even though she asks for it."

Winsome demurred, making no promises, seeing little harm. Mrs. McAllister always reimbursed her. If the niece was that concerned, let her visit her aunt more often. If Winsome had wanted to be that responsible, she would have become a school-teacher. Her mother wants her to—thinks she will change her mind after another year of bedpans and walkers—but Winsome doesn't like children enough to be with them all day. They were too dirty, nasty, and sticky for her. She despised their propensity to stick their fingers into their noses. She prefers being a home attendant, taking care of the old and infirm, who make fewer demands. She has no desire to educate the future leaders of the world.

Ernest meets her on the corner of Riverdale and Amboy in front of his uncle's laundromat.

"You late." He unhooks his change belt and hands it to another man inside.

"The woman can hardly get out of the bed. Where she going?"

"Be nice," he says, falling into step with her.

As they walk the remaining two blocks to Mrs. McAllister's apartment, he casually maneuvers her so that he is closest to the curb. Winsome pretends not to notice, but it is part of what makes her prefer him.

Entering Mrs. McAllister's apartment with her own key, Winsome steps lightly, as if in a museum, or a mausoleum. The stillness, broken only by the faint sounds coming from the TV in the back bedroom, touches something solemn in her.

"It's Winsome, ma'am," she calls out, leading Ernest by the

hand into the living room, where she peels off her coat and drops it on the hi-riser.

He whispers, "What if she comes out?"

"Don't worry, I'll hear her." Mrs. McAllister never came as far as the kitchen, and she couldn't help but make noise. Walking was difficult for the old woman since the stroke.

It took Mrs. McAllister a full ten minutes to make it down the hallway to the bathroom, her dead foot dragging along while she walk-limped.

Lying on a queen-size bed, naked except for a blanket draped over and tucked under one arm, toga-like, Mrs. McAllister is nearly motionless. With the television positioned directly in front of her, she stares into the screen. For the entire four hours Winsome is with her each day, Mrs. McAllister will remain that way, moving only to use the bathroom or switch movies out of the VCR.

"*Ghost* again?" Winsome wheels the TV stand a few inches away from the bed and hands her a cup of ginger ale.

The old woman leans on her elbow, holding the cup in her good hand. She smiles, but only one side of her mouth moves. Winsome watches her eyes for the slight lifting of the lids to find the smile. The thick fringe of Mrs. McAllister's eyelashes is so naturally dark, she looks as if she's always wearing mascara. Winsome believes she must have been beautiful once.

"Look what we have here." Winsome lays the four potato chip bags on the TV table. "Which one first?"

"Barbecue," Mrs. McAllister slurs. Winsome splits a bag along its seams and spreads it out in front of the old woman. Leaning upon one flaccid arm, Mrs. McAllister grabs at the chips, eating them greedily, licking crumbs from her orange-stained thumb and index finger.

Winsome returns to the living room. Ernest sinks into an armchair and she reaches for his zipper.

They make as little noise as possible, move as little as necessary. The apartment is silent, save for Mrs. McAllister's TV. Straddling Ernest, Winsome hears "Unchained Melody" and knows that Whoopi Goldberg and Demi Moore are embracing.

Minutes later, Mrs. McAllister's dead foot shuffles down the hallway, the good foot beside it noiselessly gliding across tile.

"Ma'am? Do you want something?" Winsome calls out.

Slowly, Mrs. McAllister's dead foot keeps coming. Winsome can feel Ernest's heart quicken against her breasts. "Let me up," he pants.

"You need me?" The question is for the old woman, but Winsome's eyes are on Ernest. If anything, the slow approach of the half-dead woman sharpens the bite of her desire.

"Yes," both he and the old woman answer. Mrs. McAllister slurs, "I have to go to the bathroom."

Ernest tries to lift her away, but Winsome places a restraining hand on his chest, no intention of stopping. "Wait, I'm coming." Refusing to free him, Winsome clenches her thighs against him, forcing his release. Taking hold of his shoulders, locking firm, she unfurls, yielding herself to the rush Mrs. McAllister will never again know.

Home Care

Thirty minutes just to prepare Mrs. McAllister for her weekly shower. Ten to help her out of the bed and out of her housedress, ten more to help her down the hallway to the bathroom, and a final ten to get her situated on her shower seat. Today was the day to bathe her, and Winsome could find no way of getting out of it.

When she arrived, she filled a basin with warm soapy water and hoped Mrs. McAllister would forget and settle for a washup instead. No sooner had she carried the kidney-shaped basin in and set it on a small tray table beside the old woman's bed than Mrs. McAllister's good hand reached out to stop her. "No," the old woman said, gripping her arm. "I'm having company today. I'll need a bath."

Winsome could barely understand her slurred speech. "What's that?"

Mrs. McAllister spoke slowly, moving the side of her mouth that had not been paralyzed by stroke. "My niece is coming to visit. I want a bath."

Winsome emptied the beige hospital-issued basin and stood to the side of the bed as Mrs. McAllister slowly worked herself up and out of it. It took some time before she was finally able to hoist herself. Using a system of rocking backward and pushing herself forward, she slowly inched herself to the edge of the bed. There she swung her good foot over, while Winsome lifted the dead one and helped her sit up. Mrs. McAllister used her good arm for leverage, pushing while Winsome pulled. Bracing her good hand against the bed, she gripped the edge of the mattress and pushed herself upward—teetering—while Winsome stood before her with open arms, waiting to catch her if she slipped and fell. As with a toddler taking her first steps, those first moments of standing were perilous. Anything within the reach of Mrs. McAllister's arm was likely to be pulled down, so Winsome moved the tray table and TV cart out of the way. Once, Mrs. McAllister had stumbled and caught Winsome around the neck, nearly strangling her. The dead hand could do nothing, but the good one was strong enough for two.

"Let's get you out of this dress," Winsome said. "Please lift your arms, ma'am."

"I can't," she said. "You know that."

"Lift the good one."

Mrs. McAllister lifted her good arm, and Winsome nudged the old woman's elbow down through the armhole of the sleeve of her striped muumuu. Even in the dead of winter, Mrs. McAllister wore these thin cotton housedresses with their round scooped necks and large patch pockets. Once they had been meant for the fastidious housewife desirous of not ruining her good clothes, but now they were worn mostly by the obese and the infirm. The bottoms of the dresses were shaped like bells, the material billowed from the waist down to camouflage girth. Held closed by front snap closures, the muumuus were simple enough that Mrs.

McAllister required very little help dressing and disrobing. With one hand she could fasten all her snaps. The muumuus were jaunty. Striped or flowered, each collar edged with satin ribbons that could be pulled and tied into a bow at the neck. Winsome preferred to see her that way—in lilac, seafoam, carnation, buttercup, and cornflower muumuus—rather than naked in the shower with her half-dead body stark and staring.

"I don't want any of those," Mrs. McAllister said. "I need something nice." She had to repeat herself twice before Winsome understood. She went to the closet where an array of Mrs. McAllister's heavy dresses waited on wire hangers, their hems hanging over useless shoes, and pulled out the first thing she saw.

"This?" The heavy dress and the matching gloves pinned to it had dulled to a pale yellow, visible even under the clear plastic.

"My old Eastern Star outfit from First AME Zion," she slurred. "No. Find something else." Winsome searched, but all the clothes were from bygone days—outdated, decaying, and boasting intricate ties, twists, sashes, and buttons—clothing Mrs. McAllister would never be able to wear again.

Her lack of suitable clothing had never before been a problem. In the two years that Winsome had been her personal home-care health aide, she'd not known Mrs. McAllister to ever go anywhere. Winsome was there four hours a day with her, and Medicare sent a nurse and physical therapist to do required checkups. Despite her hopes for the day, Mrs. McAllister never received visits from family or neighbors; she entertained no guests. Until now, the muumuus had sufficed.

Winsome settled Mrs. McAllister into her shower chair and adjusted the water. She aimed the handheld showerhead at the old woman's limbs and hosed her down. Mrs. McAllister had to be washed in sections. She was a large woman and, except for her dead limb, her body was strong. There was an unnerving solidity to her at times like this when Winsome showered her, a radiating warmth that rose from the stale bedridden skin that smelled of sheets and sweat and sleep. Mrs. McAllister's body would keep her alive much longer than she wished. Winsome marveled at its tenacity as she passed the soapy washcloth under and over the sagging breasts. Unlike other clients her age, there was no papery wrinkling of the skin, no flimsiness to the flesh, no sign that the flesh beneath was losing hold of its clutch on life and skin and bone and hair.

"Is this niece the one I met before?"

"That was Marcia, my sister's daughter. This is my great-niece Ellen. I used to take care of her; she lived with me. She's in college. She's smart. You've seen her picture."

Alone in the living room where Mrs. McAllister could no longer go, Winsome had seen the lone picture on the mantel among the dead and dying plants she was not paid to water. Mrs. McAllister had several times had her retrieve albums from the top of her closet and shown her old pictures of her with her parents and siblings, but Winsome did not care for those photographs. Dating back to the late thirties, they were black-and-white pictures, older than old. Winsome did not care to see Mrs. McAllister's father in his military uniform or Mrs. McAllister's mother in a studio shot with a fake fox fur thrown over her shoulder or Mrs. McAllister herself standing in the middle of five other children dressed for church with her ankle socks drooping, squinting into the sun. Those pictures made her seem historical, made it seem as if she were already dead.

Born two years after the stock market crash in 1929, she had already seen more life than Winsome had read of in school.

Those pictures made Winsome place Mrs. McAllister in the annals of all the American history her mother had made her study when they'd first arrived from Jamaica and discovered the insignificance of British deeds of valor. Yes, she had seen the picture of Mrs. McAllister's niece. She had often been drawn to it. Drawn to the bamboo wicker chair the young girl sat in that Winsome recognized so well from her own picture day at school, the wicker chair that dated the photograph and helped Winsome place it in the late eighties. She had sat in such a chair for her fourth-grade picture, the first school picture she'd ever taken in the United States. She'd been quickly ushered into the seat by the harassed photographer who was eager to get to the other thirty or so children who waited. She'd only been allowed to sit and pose for two minutes, but she'd wanted to remain in the seat that felt so much like a throne and seemed so much like a promise made to her of what her life would be now that they had left Kingston and Jamaica behind.

Yes, she had seen the picture and the young girl who sat dwarfed in that wicker chair, whose long black hair looked as if it had been pressed and curled for just such an event, whose eyes met the camera head-on with a confidence that Winsome's own frightened stare did not reveal, whose legs did not reach the bottom of the chair, who must even now be three or four inches shorter than herself. Once gone, a girl like that would not return to Brooklyn so easily. Not for a half-dead great-aunt. Yes, she had seen the picture. She had been drawn to it and to the girl she did not know but who must surely be near in age to her, who was now off in college while she herself had merely taken a certificate and was forced to share a bedroom with her nosy younger sister. Her own mother would have never let her travel far for something like school, which could be had anywhere.

Mrs. McAllister said, "You're scrubbing too hard."

"Sorry," she said, "there's a lot of dirt."

"My niece and I used to play hangman on my back," the old woman said. "Ellen would rub lotion over my back and then write in it and I'd have to guess whatever she had spelled."

Winsome soaped and rinsed Mrs. McAllister's dead arm.

"She always did it in print. I couldn't guess it if she did it in cursive," Mrs. McAllister said.

Winsome poured liquid soap on the rough washcloth and guided it from one side to the other across Mrs. McAllister's expansive back, making it something other than a dead thing. The filmy soap transformed her skin into a chalkboard. Winsome started at the left and, working her way to the right shoulder blade, she traced a sentence across the old woman's back, letters of skin appearing through lather. *No one is coming.*

After some time, Mrs. McAllister said, "I can't make it out."

Winsome retraced her letters in the too-quickly dissolving lather, but the old woman refused to play.

"Water's getting cold," Mrs. McAllister complained.

Winsome adjusted the water, aimed the showerhead at her handiwork, and washed away the truth from Mrs. McAllister's back.

Mrs. McAllister

It was colder than he remembered; he felt the bite of the wind, sharp against his ears. He shoved his hands into his unlined pockets as he forcefully turned the corner against the wind. He had come home.

The ground was the same beneath his feet. The same sidewalk from fifteen years before. The street sign had changed from Hopkinson Avenue to Thomas S. Boyland Street. He didn't know who Thomas S. Boyland was, nor did anyone in the community, but he was sure that this T. S. Boyland had not done a thing for them. No one had.

As a child, he'd ignored the empty lot across the street. It was fenced up, as if it would soon be worked on. That fence had been there since he could remember.

Before, broken wheels, old clothes, discarded toys, and shopping carts filled it. Now, forty-ounce beer bottles, small ziplock bags, packs of cigarettes, brown paper bags, Chinese food cartons, used condoms, and broken razors vied with the old garbage. Multicolored crack vials, with their black, red, white, blue, green, and yellow tops, blinked at him under the sun like Christmas lights out of season. Brownsville had never seemed so different, so remote.

Garbage bags lay at the corners, waiting to be picked up, overflowing and rewarding the sidewalk with filthy treasure.

The wind blew him down the street with great, lusty gusts. Without much hope, he looked up to the window on the corner. There she was. Her fleshy arms, the color of corn bread, were propped against the pane. Mrs. McAllister. He remembered her and her untamed head that dropped straight into her arms with no apparent neck as a go-between. Her eyes were not on him; as always, she looked out and over the projects and rows of identical apartments and streets. He guessed she probably didn't even see the lot across the street. Her hair was as wild as ever, an Afro with no shape to it; it was uneven on one side, most likely slept on, an untamed, uncombed shock of steely gray with sightings of black peppering through. Her hair blew every which way like the shade above her whenever she nodded her head. The shade slapped the glass, lightly blown by every small breeze, coming apart in defiance of the mailing tape that haphazardly patched it together in zigzags. She had never bought a new shade for her window. Mrs. McAllister hadn't changed at all.

He and his friends spent their summer vacations sitting on her stoop. Beneath her window, they were protected from New York's summer heat and choking air. Sitting on her railings, with no hands they kicked out and leaned as far back as they could without falling. It was always a feat to jump onto the concrete garbage bin in one leap instead of using the footholds that were the door's hinges. Or sometimes they just played a boom box and talked trash. In the middle of their fun, her tirade breathed down their necks, as if she had spoken out loud, but without a word. *Can't even walk down the steps without stepping on one of them. Why don't they go sit on their own stoops, dirty that up?* On cue, one of them would crack a sunflower seed between his teeth, spit the shell out and say, "Sure is a good thing people don't pay rent on stoops."

This was their spot, and they weren't about to leave. They could see everything from their vantage point on that stoop. Four blocks down were the public school with the free lunch program and the minimarket run by Dominicans who were ready to fight if you called them Puerto Rican or Spanish. They could see up to Brookdale Hospital and the other public school—the one that didn't offer free lunch. To the left, two more blocks of Marcus Garvey Village housing projects, apartments identical to their own. Another empty lot and a fenced-off basketball court that led to the Key Food supermarket. From Mrs. McAllister's stoop, they could see their whole world, and they owned all that they surveyed.

And girls. They could see all the pretty girls who passed by from the trains or buses or the public pool or Betsy Head Park on their way to the supermarket or the Laundromat or the beauty salon or the pizza shop—they all passed in front of the stoop to get to where they were going. They would call out to the girls—usually nicely, but not always—watching them walk by, swishing their high ponytails meant to keep the hair out of their faces and off their necks, or swinging the braids that fell against their shoulders and backs with light lapping sounds. They took in everything from the tight cutoff Daisy Dukes with the frayed denim fringes that barely covered the girls' brown legs and instead left them big and bare—Calvin Klein had nothing on these girls—to the slight sucking sound their shoes made as they walked and their heels slapped against their flip-flops. They inhaled the sweet scent of baby powder dusted lightly under arms, across the fronts of tube tops, behind necks and knees that wafted up through the air like seduction.

After the girls passed, they would talk about them. Their words came off thickly, nervously in whispers and stutters peppered with anxious silences. They couldn't talk like they wanted; they didn't want *her* to hear. Mrs. McAllister was in the window as always. They wished she would just duck her head in and mind her own business.

Then they would be ashamed because Mrs. McAllister had probably heard them, and she *did* mind her business. She'd never once told their mothers that they lit firecrackers and threw them into the street at people and cats. Or that they spray-painted her door and stoop with their tag names. She never told that they smoked beneath her window and that they left sunflower seeds strewn all over the steps of the stoop.

He looked up again at her. Her woolly head, tilted down, held him in regard. He wanted to tell her that he didn't do those things anymore, but all he said was hello. She said nothing, just nodded, but standing there under her regard, he was made small again. He was lanky and awkward again, all bony legs and ashy knees. He was brought back to that stoop, to being a boy with skinny legs and long feet smoothly leaping and gaining the garbage bin with one foot and no hands, to calling the girl he liked bad names so that his friends would not know he liked her, or want her for themselves, and to looking up to the window and seeing that woolly head nodding toward him, silently.

What Is Left Undone

Mrs. McAllister was nobody's fool. She'd just missed being born on April Fool's Day, arriving shortly after midnight, mere minutes making the difference. No one had ever been able to put anything past her. Not her younger sisters when she'd been put in charge and they'd tried to test her authority. Not her coworkers when she'd worked the till for Rosen's and the night's figures didn't add up right. Not even her husband when he'd claimed to be working late, yet his pay stubs showed no additional pay.

So why did the housegirl think she could fool her? The young Jamaican woman who was Mrs. McAllister's home attendant was responsible for preparing light meals, running errands, and helping Mrs. McAllister bathe and complete her physical therapy exercises. She was also there for company, meant to help stave off the loneliness that came with being old and infirm, but Mrs. McAllister didn't make the girl dance attention on her. Instead, she let the housegirl get away with washing her only once a week and she allowed her to spend most of her shift in the living room, where she was meant to believe the girl sat on the couch for hours reading for certifications and exams, but where she instead brought her boyfriend and engaged in clandestine sex. Somehow,

Mrs. McAllister wasn't supposed to know when another person was in her apartment or hear the extra set of footsteps—heavy, plodding—that could belong only to a man, since the housegirl wore rubber-soled shoes like the nurses over at Brookdale and walked noiselessly. Somehow, Mrs. McAllister wasn't supposed to notice that for all the studying the housegirl claimed to do, she had never so much as brought to her shift a single book.

She blamed the key for the girl's sly antics. Mrs. McAllister had taken pity on her, not wanting to leave the girl out on the stoop waiting in all kinds of weather for an old woman to make her slow way to opening the door. It took Mrs. McAllister a good ten minutes to navigate the short hallway from her bedroom to the door of the apartment and to buzz the intercom to unlock the outer door downstairs, and even longer to steady her hands enough to open the front door. When her family used to visit, they'd buzz the intercom and wait on the stoop for her to come to the window and throw out the keys, dropping them right at their feet. She'd tried that with the girl, but now her grip was weak and her aim was off—when she threw down the keys they landed on top of the concrete garbage bin and nowhere near the housegirl. Though her family didn't know it, Mrs. McAllister had long since given the housegirl her own key, and for some time now the girl had been letting herself in.

Today the housegirl had come alone but she didn't stay for long. When she brought Mrs. McAllister her lunch, she'd spun a sad tale about an ill relative and warned that she might have to leave early if called for. An hour later, just as the girl was retrieving the lunch dishes, the intercom sounded. Without answering it, the housegirl said, "That must be for me, ma'am. My cousin Hedda said she might come and fetch me. May I go?"

Not for a second did Mrs. McAllister believe her. A female

cousin? With the housegirl so dolled up? With the girl's face so heavily powdered in makeup five shades too light for her complexion, her lips caked so thick with layers of cheap red lipstick, and her body so doused in cloying drugstore perfume? With her usually sullen demeanor gone and her standing there in the bedroom's doorway, radiating with anticipation, aglow with expectation and the surety of a much-desired thing?

Mrs. McAllister said only, "The dishes?"

The girl looked at the plate in her hand and the bowl in the other without recognition. She came to and said, "Yes, I'll take care of it and then I'll go," but minutes later Mrs. McAllister heard the dishes clatter in the sink, followed by the sound of the front door slamming closed.

What a bold and foolish girl to take such chances and risk her job for a man! Mrs. McAllister hoped the young man was worth it but couldn't imagine how he could be. She had married one man and loved another, and only one of them had ever been worth taking any kind of risk, but perhaps the housegirl didn't think her behavior risky at all. Surely, she presumed herself safe from discovery—after all, Mrs. McAllister never ventured past the kitchen, and never took those final few steps to the living room to see for herself what the housegirl did or did not do.

Thoughts of the undone dishes nagged at Mrs. McAllister. She thought to watch a movie, but she couldn't concentrate after pressing play on the VCR. The sink was by no means full—the dishes consisted of one plate, one bowl, and one set of utensils. Not much at all, yet the thought of them sitting idly in the basin of her kitchen sink and attracting flies worried her. Had the girl at least run water over them? Had she wiped down the counter

for crumbs? Had she left out all the food she'd used to prepare
lunch? Had she rewrapped the cold cuts, screwed the lid back
on the jar of mayonnaise, closed the tie on the bag of bread, and
resealed the cheese? These weren't things Mrs. McAllister nor-
mally worried over, but today the housegirl had been so aflutter
and distracted that she resolved to check for herself. She couldn't
wash the dishes, but if she took her time and used the kitchen
counters for balance, she might be able to put the other things
away. She would store the dirty dishes in the vegetable bin and
the girl could wash them the next day, but the food left out on the
counter really couldn't wait.

It took some time for Mrs. McAllister to get moving. Getting
her good arm and leg to cooperate and carry the dead side of her
body was more than a notion. She rolled herself forward and back
in her bed until she generated enough momentum to grab on to
the TV cart for leverage and sit herself up. This was all easier to
do when the housegirl was there to push while she pulled, but
eventually Mrs. McAllister managed to swing her feet over the
edge of the bed. It didn't matter that she could only feel her good
foot when she slipped on her house shoes—all that mattered was
what she planned to do. The idea to wash the dishes herself did
not come upon her all at once, but by the time she was standing
Mrs. McAllister was convinced of her own strength. After she
put away the kitchen items she *would* do those dishes—it would
be good therapy for her hands. Perhaps she could use the good
hand to wash and the dead hand to dry. Perhaps she could do it
without using the dead hand at all. Perhaps, when it was all done,
she could sit in her living room, which she had long since abandoned. She had not been in the living room for years—not since
she'd first been assigned a home attendant. After the stroke, she'd
found the going back and forth from one end of the apartment to

the other too tiring and had her family move the television into her bedroom, but there were other things she could enjoy out there. There was her hi-fi stereo system and though the eight-track player was broken, the turntable and radio portions were still good. The housegirl never touched the hi-fi—she was too young to know how to work it. The last person who'd played that stereo had been her great-niece Ellen, home on a break from boarding school. If Mrs. McAllister could make it as far as the living room, she could sit down on the loveseat near the hi-fi and turn on the radio. The tuner's dial would be on the last station Ellen had listened to, and if she sat there and listened to it too, it would be just like having her back home again.

Halfway down the hallway, just between the bedroom and the bathroom, Mrs. McAllister felt her good leg tremble, weakening on her. She paused and braced herself against the hall closet, willing strength into her good side. Ever since the stroke, she'd only been able to make it down the hall to the kitchen, and even that took time and effort—she's never had the stamina, the leg or arm strength, to make it farther. Her bedroom was only a few short steps away, but that would mean turning back, which Mrs. McAllister was determined not to do. She would need to sit in her living room and rest after standing for so long.

The housegirl was supposed to help her practice her walking. Together, during each of the girl's shifts, they were supposed to walk twice up and down the length of the apartment from the bedroom to the living room, but they'd only ever practiced once. Mrs. McAllister remembered that one time well, how the willowy West Indian girl had gripped her dead arm and tried to slow her own step to match an old woman's gait, yet still ended up eclipsing her. She remembered that when she'd called a halt, slurring, "No more," they had just passed the hallway closet, not even going as far down the hall as the bathroom—a distance Mrs. McAllister knew she could make. She had wanted to go no farther. With the girl's arm wound through hers like that, it had felt too much to her like walking down the aisle—too much like giving herself away.

Yet she had never actually walked down an aisle. Mrs. McAllister had been married in the parlor of a building owned by the Eastern Stars, just a few streets away from the block where she used to live. Her brother, a Mason, had given her away. Her young niece, a knobby-kneed ten-year-old girl, had stood up with her and acted as best man because Roland had just come over from Kingston and didn't know anyone in this country other than the woman he had been brought over to marry.

Mrs. McAllister gathered her strength and made it past the bathroom, where she leaned against the door and took another break. After some time, she made it to the kitchen. There she was glad to see that no food had been left out. It was only the dishes that needed to be done, but she was too tired now to even try. She looked forward to having a seat. A few steps more would take her where she longed to go.

When Mrs. McAllister's leg went out from under her there was no one to help steady her or catch her before she fell. And there was no one to help her up. The floor beneath her was cold but not unclean. She closed her eyes against the glare from the hallway light overhead. She couldn't feel her body. She'd grown used to missing the left side, but now her entire body seemed to disappear beneath her. Soon she couldn't even feel the cold floor. Something in her brain pulsed and flickered like the flimsy filament in a dying bulb.

She knew that she would not be able to get up without help. There was nothing near enough on to which she could grab hold—no door handle, no kitchen counter, no chair to be her crutch and help her scrabble to her feet. There was nothing she could do but wait. Tomorrow, the housegirl would come. She'd let herself in and she'd find the old woman on the cold hallway floor and the dishes in the sink, which she, in all her hurry, had carelessly left undone.

Long Time Coming

Some Fridays Eunice McAllister could have to herself. That's when she would pick up a strawberry cheesecake from Junior's and come straight home without making any other stops. Carrying the red-and-white-striped box by its knotted string, she'd turn the corner of MacDonough Street, make her way down the block past a few houses and then the stoops of three identical apartment buildings to reach 32, and everyone who saw her would know there was no party that night. The cheesecake was meant just for herself, her mother, the niece she had care of, and her sister and nephews in the apartment below. After Eunice had cut the cheesecake and sent off her niece to deliver the slices, she'd hand over money to her mother, and then settle in the living room and turn on the television to watch the Million Dollar Movie, which more often than not was *Rachel and the Stranger*. She'd prop her tired feet atop the coffee table and turn on channel 9 just in time for the opening shot of sleepy-eyed Robert Mitchum, dressed all in fringed buckskin, singing and strumming his guitar as he stalked through the wilderness. She ignored her family's teasing, shut out their reminders that she lived in Bedford-Stuyvesant and not on the frontier of the Old West. She swooned over

Robert Mitchum and William Holden, but it was for Loretta Young's Rachel that Eunice watched the movie again and again. She felt kinship with the white bondswoman whom no one ever saw as anything more than labor and who had been forced to become an indentured servant to lift the burden of debt from her family.

Eunice was never meant to be the family's oldest girl. She was the third-born of six children, born after her brother Edsel and her sister Mabel. She became the oldest girl by default when Mabel died at the hands of the incompetent doctor she'd sought out when she found herself in trouble with nowhere to turn. One evening Mabel said she was going to the Bijou to see a movie with friends, but instead she'd bled and hemorrhaged and died all alone. When the mantle passed to Eunice, she did her duty. She took a job at the Banco, working part-time at the local movie theater until she finished high school. On Sundays, after church, she'd take the train up to Manhattan to window-shop on the Lower East Side, where the stores were open. She'd checked out all the bargains on Delancey Street and was walking up toward the Bowery when she passed in front of a jeweler's and the owner stepped outside and called to her. Mr. Rosen had been looking to employ a colored girl to work in his shop and he liked the look of her. Struck by her bearing—her neat dress, light skin, and fine dark eyes—he offered her a job right on the spot. The GIs were back now and keen to marry their sweethearts, and he predicted that the colored soldiers would take one look at her statuesque beauty and spend, spend, spend. For seventeen years now, half of her life, Eunice had been working for Rosen's, bringing money home to her mother every Friday evening and telling herself she was happy.

———

But most Fridays didn't go that way, and instead of coming home to a quiet evening of self-pity, cheesecake, and a movie, Eunice came home to an apartment full of people. The night before, her mother would declare herself in the mood for company, and word of the coming card party would spread. Her mother and two of her sisters, Myrtle and Geraldine, would spend the day cooking and preparing platters to sell to the people who came to play pitty-pat for money. Her mother's Eastern Star sisters came with heavy purses and loose change. Eunice's brother brought his Masons. Men came from Tompkins Avenue, from Gates, from Marcy, even over from Albany Avenue to partake of her mother's card parties and ogle the McAllister girls, who were lure enough. On these Friday evenings when she knew her mother and sisters were setting up, Eunice found it easier to stay out of the way until everything was ready. Instead of coming straight home she'd stop in at King's Corner bar, which she had to pass on her way from the subway station to her home. Just across the street from Restoration Plaza, the bar was cool and quiet in the early evening, and there she would sit nursing her drink—always a Harvey Wallbanger—among the other slumped workers until someone was sent to find her to come break up the fight.

That time, they sent Lucas.

There she was sitting, comfortable at the bar, decompressing from a day on her feet, contemplating the bright, citrusy drink she had barely touched, when Lucas came in, letting in all the early evening light behind him. When the shaft of light threw itself across the bar counter, she turned to see him standing there, tall and anxious, hat low over his eyes, searching for her.

When he saw her, he touched the brim of his hat, nodded, and said, "Miss Mac wants you right away. Your sister's fighting again."

The highball glass was still mostly full, but Eunice threw back her drink and told Old Cleo to put it on her tab. She wasn't dressed for running, so she walked at a fast clip, Lucas easily outpacing her. She didn't need to ask who was fighting—if they wanted her to break it up, she already knew.

Geraldine and Johnnie Mae would be fighting over Donald, Eunice's brother-in-law. Last summer, he'd married her baby sister, Mildred, who was now expecting, but before he'd courted Mildred, he'd fathered a child with Johnnie Mae, who lived over in the 28 building. Whenever Eunice's family threw a party, Johnnie Mae caused trouble. As soon as she'd see Eunice's brother carrying up bags of ice, she'd come outside and perch on her stoop with her three-year-old daughter, a pop-eyed girl who was the spitting image of Donald. When Eunice's young, innocent, and pregnant sister showed up, Johnnie Mae would taunt her to tears. Their mother had told them to let it alone—Donald and Johnnie Mae were old news; he had not even met Mildred when his little girl was born. All but Geraldine complied. Whenever Johnnie Mae sent Mildred up the stairs crying, Geraldine would come downstairs to clean the woman's clock.

A crowd had converged on the sidewalk in front of the stoop. Eunice tried to part the thick crowd of onlookers, knowing her sister didn't need much time to get her licks in. Geraldine didn't waste time arguing or reasoning, she just swung and threw punches. She had already whupped Johnnie Mae on multiple occasions, but their neighbor kept coming back for more.

By the time Eunice faced the two women, Johnnie Mae's lip was bleeding, and her hair was wild and in disarray. Her dress was hanging off one shoulder and she had lost a shoe. Geraldine wasn't even winded.

"Gerri, that's enough!" Eunice threw herself between the

two women. She was hoping to keep them apart long enough to give Johnnie Mae a chance to run, but upon catching her breath, Johnnie Mae edged closer. Geraldine sidestepped Eunice and forced the woman into a headlock.

"She's had enough!" Eunice tried to pry her sister's arms loose.

"Not nearly. She's going to shut her mouth or I'm going to shut it for her!"

"Just let her go," Eunice said. "You want to kill her?"

Her sister tightened her grip. Johnnie Mae's arms flailed wildly, and her face got redder and redder.

"Please, Gerri," Eunice said. "Please."

Eunice looked back at the crowd, knowing no one would intervene and help her. The women and children were all too fascinated, and none of the men would dare step in and be accused of manhandling a woman. Lucas was at the edge of the crowd, leaning against the fire hydrant, but when she beckoned, he shook his head. He pantomimed the act of eating and rubbed his fingers in a gesture for payment.

"Mama wants us upstairs," she coaxed, thankful for his hint. "You know she needs our help selling all those platters."

With that her sister released Johnnie Mae. She stood over the coughing, sputtering, crumpled woman and said, "Let this be the last time I have to tell you. Leave my baby sister alone."

Lucas ushered the two sisters inside to their mother's party, which was just beginning. For the rest of the evening, he stayed close. At first Eunice thought it simple courtesy, but even when the party was in full swing, he was never far from her side. All evening long he teased, calling her umpire and referee for breaking up the fight. He had come to the card party with three other fellows, and after introductions the men dispersed, purchasing their meals and then milling around the apartment, eating and drinking, occasionally sitting in on a hand to spell one of the more serious card players, while Lucas stayed glued to her side. She'd heard that he'd been walking out with Suze, a thin yellow girl with birdlike features who lived over on Albany Avenue, but his behavior made that seem untrue. Lucas stood nearby as she helped her sister serve the platters. He followed her into the kitchen when she went for more ice to replenish the drinks, and when she went to take over at the record player he sorted through the 45s and handed her the ones she requested.

She'd just finished playing Marvin Gaye's "Ain't That Peculiar" and had flipped the record over to its B side for "She's Got to Be Real" when Lucas pulled her away from the hi-fi. He led her to a corner of the room where he found a single folding chair and insisted that she sit. "You need to take a break," he said. He remained standing, shielding her from the crowd. "You've done your share for the evening, Ref."

"You could have helped me pull Johnnie Mae loose."

"Not with Gerri turning her every which way *but* loose." Lucas laughed at his own joke. "You're the only one with enough fire to handle Gerri. Your sister really packs a wallop."

Fire? What fire did she have, Eunice wondered. He was mistaken if he thought her actions stemmed from bravery rather than duty. She was only doing what was necessary and obeying her mother's request. "Not me," she said. "No fire for me."

"You're the only one who could have talked Gerri down."

"What's so brave about talking?"

"That was only your first option. She knows that you could have taken her."

Eunice protested, "I would never fight my sister."

"Maybe not, but if you did, you would beat her. She knows that. Miss Mac knows too. Myrtle and Mildred would fold. That's why they always send for you. Not just because you're the oldest of the four."

But Lucas had it wrong. She could not beat Geraldine if she tried; her sister was tougher than anyone Eunice had ever known. She'd been abandoned by her husband in another state, left behind in Connecticut, and yet she'd come back home to Brooklyn stronger than ever. She didn't whine or complain about having three young children to provide for, no, instead she spread her wide wings and folded their baby sister under her protection as well. Eunice never wanted to go up against such grit. Lucas was wrong about that, just as he was wrong about her being the oldest and the sisters numbering only four.

"You still could have helped," she said.

"Miss Mac gave me one job. She did not give me permission to lay a hand on any of her girls. She would probably kill me if I so much as touched one of her precious daughters." His eyes drifted over her, roaming her face. He stretched out a hand toward her cheek, reaching but not touching. Eunice tilted slightly forward, leaning into his caress. "Precious, precious indeed."

Lucas led her to the floor, already crowded with couples. Barbara Mason's "Yes, I'm Ready" played on the hi-fi, which meant that her sister Myrtle had taken charge of the music and there'd be only slow songs for the rest of the evening.

Lucas said, "You know, you all could be rich if Miss Mac would just sell tickets to one of Gerri's fights!" and Eunice felt the rumble of his laughter against her.

"You should tell her that."

"Maybe I will," he whispered. "It's not such a bad idea. You all could be living the life of Riley."

"That'd be nice," she said. "No more card parties."

His arms tightened around her. "Then again, maybe I won't tell her."

Someone put on a new record. Lucas pulled her in, arms circling her waist as Sam Cooke sang of being born by the river and predicted that a change would come. All around them couples were slow dragging, and no one took notice of them dancing together, just as no one had noticed his constant presence at her side after bringing her back from breaking up the fight. There in a crowded apartment in a tenement on a block where she had lived her whole life and thought there was nothing left for her to discover, she learned how a simple touch could awaken her and make her see the world in a new light, could shift all the things she thought she knew. Lucas had stopped laughing and joking, stopped talking altogether, and now just held her close. They didn't need to talk at all any longer. The song was in their ears and their hearts were in the song and listening was the best that they could do and all one ever need do and they would never need any more words between them because all the words there were had all been said and they danced there, two throbbing, listening hearts, and each breath was a beat and each beat was a breath and however they moved forward in life from this moment on, they would always know. Yes, they would always know.

Keepsake

The last time you saw Lucas was shortly after your mother passed. Although your family had long since moved off the block, with the funeral held at First AME Zion, on the corner of the street where you grew up, everyone from the old neighborhood showed up to bid your mother farewell. It had been years since you had seen each other, not since you called it quits and married other people. Lucas attended the service with his wife and his children. He didn't speak to you inside the church or at the gravesite. After the interment, he took his family home and came alone to the wake.

At the wake, held in the apartment you and your mother had moved to on Riverdale Avenue, Lucas cut through the swath of your sisters and drew you out of the small apartment, down the hallway, and outside onto the stoop. He spread his suit jacket on the top step so that you could sit. "Miss Mac meant a lot to all of us," he said. "I hope you don't think I was wrong to come."

"No, I appreciate it. We all do. Thank you, Lucas." You turned toward the railing and the street. One of the cars parked in front of your building bore a Jackson '84 bumper sticker and you were saddened by the knowledge that if Jesse Jackson won and became the first black president, your mother wouldn't be there to see it.

"Your mother was the kindest lady," he said.

"Yes."

"Nobody will ever be like her."

"No."

Lucas wasn't telling you anything you didn't already know. The apartment above was filled with former neighbors recounting the goodness of your mother, marveling that she had passed on April 22, Easter Sunday, which they considered recompense and a just reward for a life so faithfully lived. Your mother was beloved by everyone who knew her, but most of all by you. And now, for the first time you were alone. All your life you had been a daughter and now you were . . . not. You were the oldest girl, the one tasked with supporting the family, corralling your sisters, and providing them with a shoulder to cry on. You were meant to keep everyone and everything together, but you were full of unshed tears.

Lucas was the only one who noticed. He sat beside you and nudged you closer to the railing, where you were farther out of view and lost behind his broad shoulders. "No one can see you," he promised, and you pressed your cheek against his back and cried. Soothed by his silence and the cool cotton of his shirt, that release was just what you'd needed, and how like Lucas to know.

But that's how it was between the two of you. One evening during the summer of 1966, Lucas had been sent to fetch you from a bar to have you break up a fight, and that was all it took for you to recognize each other and become inseparable. He'd been walking out with a girl named Suze, but after that night they parted ways and he devoted all his time and attention to you. For so long Lucas was your every thought and his name the only sound you knew. He expected you to marry him and couldn't believe it when you said no or when you told him that you never wanted to have children. He'd been willing to wait, to let you take all the time you needed, hopeful you'd change your mind, unaware of what prompted your decision and how unlikely you were to reconsider.

No one in your family ever talked with others about Mabel, who died at the age of sixteen. Although it was not uncommon for a girl in trouble to go south for a visit among relatives and return months later healthier and happier, all your people had left North Carolina ages ago, slowly making their way up north until everyone lived within a few blocks of each other in Bedford-Stuyvesant on MacDonough Street or over on Gates or Tompkins Avenues, so there wasn't anywhere safe for your sister to go. Mabel's death had not stopped any of your other sisters from having children, but they had not shared a bed with her, had not slept beside her night after night, falling asleep to the sound of her tears. The mattress had not trembled beneath them when she couldn't stop crying, even in her troubled sleep. They had never wrapped their arms around her, hugged her from behind, soothed and patted her off to slumber, and had to pretend the next morning that the night had never happened. You and your siblings each received a lock of Mabel's hair for a keepsake, but you didn't need a token to remember her, since she was never far from your thoughts. How could she be, when you had taken her place as the eldest girl and were living the life that was meant to be hers?

When you were all cried out, Lucas turned to face you. With his thumbs he dried your tears. Thankfully, he didn't bring up the past as you sat together on the stoop, though it would have been all too easy to do so. Lucas asked about your family, wanted to know where everyone had moved to, and wondered how everyone was holding up. He asked you to pass him the sunglasses in his inner coat pocket, and though it was the end of April and not at all sunny, he sighed as soon as he slid them on. With his shades on he reminded you of Ray Charles, whom he'd taken you to see at the Apollo Theater back in 1968. Had things been different, you might have teased him about the resemblance, but such thoughts disappeared when he tapped the hinge of his sunglasses and said, "I'm losing my sight."

He said it was just a matter of time, that his doctor predicted that he'd be blind a year from now, or maybe in just a few months. How you wished you had said something comforting, but you couldn't speak above the swell of pity lumped in your throat, couldn't imagine this man who was all brightness being lost to a life in the dark. You took his hand and squeezed it, crying fresh new tears. He said, "After all that we've been to each other, I wanted to see your face one last time before I'm never able to see it again."

"Then it's a shame you have to see me like this," you said, opting for levity, as you wiped your runny nose. But Lucas saw past the effects of your crying. "You've never been anything less than beautiful to me," he said.

How wrong you were to give him up! How selfless you thought yourself when you urged him to return to Suze while you devoted yourself to caring for your mother and buried yourself in raising your niece. Lucas was strong, healthy, and virile—he had every right to want and expect a marriage that produced children, and you could never believe that you would ever be enough. You didn't hold it against him when he did eventually marry Suze. You didn't begrudge him for seeking the life that you wouldn't ever have been able to give him—you were the one who threw away the chance to mean something in his life. And when he named his fourth child—his second daughter—Eunice, you thought it the nicest way to share a child with him. You married later in life when children were no longer an option, after your cousin

Arletta matched you to Roland Simpson, a man she'd met in Jamaica where she'd gone on a cruise. She'd showed him a picture of you and her at your sister Mildred's wedding and he'd been immediately smitten. She'd vouched for him, told you that he was handsome and hardworking; she was sure the two of you would suit. Though you and Lucas had floundered after splitting, you'd both married others and managed to find your way. Yet the truth of that matter was that Lucas had never truly forgiven you for giving up and letting him go. And, for that matter, neither had you.

So, now when the intercom buzzes short and zappy like a secret code you're meant to recognize, you figure it can only be him. Who else could it be? The housegirl, your home attendant, has a key and has already gone for the day. Your great-niece Ellen has one too, so you know it isn't her. Ever since she'd left for college, her visits have become rare and rarer still. No one else in your family would drop by without first calling, and the Jehovah's Witnesses wouldn't dare.

Surely, it must be Lucas with his way of showing up just when you need him, like now when you have fallen, like the woman in the old commercial, and cannot get up on your own. It makes perfect sense to you that it's Lucas downstairs, ringing your bell, even though he's been dead for some time. You can forgive him for dying if he can forgive you for everything else.

There it is again—that buzzing, ringing sound. You make an effort to rise. It's a struggle and it takes some time, but eventually you find purchase, holding on to the doorknob to get to your feet, and pull yourself up. You step over your body where it lies prone on the hallway floor, determined not to keep him waiting. You open the door and there Lucas stands, holding a lock of your sister's hair.

Notes

"What She Finds" first appeared in *Peauxdunque Review*.

"Buen Provecho" first appeared in *The Los Angeles Review*.

"Quarter Rican" first appeared in *Latino Book Review*.

"Rerun" first appeared in *Kweli*.

"What the Mouth Knows" first appeared in *Craft*.

"We Ask Why" first appeared in *Able Muse*.

"That Island" first appeared in *Write City*.

"What the Tide Returns" first appeared in *American Short Fiction*.

"Feliz Navidad" first appeared in *The Cincinnati Review*.

"Thankful Chinese" first appeared in *Southeast Review*.

"Before" first appeared in *Quarterly West*.

"Surely Not" first appeared in *Boston Review*.

"You'll Go" first appeared in *Literary Matters*.

"We Wonder (Ode to Lisa Lisa)" first appeared in *Love in the Time of Time's Up*, ed. Christine Sneed.

"Preferences" first appeared in *Pindledyboz*.

"Kitler" first appeared in *Oxford American*.

"My Mother Wins an Oxygen Tank at the Casino, or, My Mother Makes an Exception" first appeared in *Gulf Coast*.

"Everything" first appeared in *Blackbird*.

"So Good to See You" first appeared in *Hypertext Magazine*.

"Forgive Me" first appeared in *TriQuarterly*.

"Dutch" first appeared in *Blackbird*.

"Why Not?" first appeared in *Literary Matters*.

"Come Sunday" first appeared in *Studio Magazine*.

"Childhood, Princesshood, Motherhood" first appeared in *Blackbird*.

"Hunger Memory" first appeared in *Crab Orchard Review*.

"Howl" first appeared in *Literary Matters*.

"The Best That You Can Do" first appeared in *Quarter After Eight*.

"Diminishing Returns" first appeared in *Pleiades*.

"A Recipe for Curry" first appeared in *New Century Voices*.

"Brat" first appeared in *Nelle*.

"Minnow" first appeared in *River Styx*.

"Second Sally" first appeared in *The Hong Kong Review*.

"Doing It" first appeared in *B&A: New Fiction*.

"Slip" first appeared in *Mississippi Review*.

"Prone" first appeared in *The Southeast Review*.

"Value Judgments" first appeared in *Potpourri*.

"Pursed" first appeared in *New Flash Fiction Review*.

"Don't Mention It" first appeared in *Blackbird*.

"Breathe" first appeared in *Notre Dame Review*.

"Discotheque of Negroes" first appeared in *Southwest Review*.

"Elevator" first appeared in *Pleiades*.

"Tears on Tap" first appeared in *Passages North*.

"Mean to Me" first appeared in *Southeast Review*.

"Karen" first appeared in *Sycamore Review*.

"Monument" first appeared in *Raleigh Review*.

"Dismissal" first appeared in *TriQuarterly*.

"Housegirl" first appeared in *StoryQuarterly*.

"Caretaking" first appeared in *Cerise Journal*.

"Home Care" first appeared in *Torch*.

"Mrs. McAllister" first appeared in *African Voices*.

Amina Gautier, Ph.D., is the author of three short story collections: *At-Risk*, *Now We Will Be Happy*, and *The Loss of All Lost Things*. Gautier is the recipient of the Blackwell Prize, the Chicago Public Library Foundation's 21st Century Award, the International Latino Book Award, the Flannery O'Connor Award, and the Phillis Wheatley Award in Fiction. For her body of work, she has received the PEN/Malamud Award for Excellence in the Short Story.